IN THE HEAVENS
OF DEATH

The monstrous flying reptile had noted my fall from the balloon's basket, and now as I swung temptingly to and fro, the winged horror made a savage stab at me.

Fanged jaws snapped sickeningly close as the thing whirled by. And as it veered away, one great black bat-like wing dealt me a terrific blow.

Stunned for a moment, my grip on the line loosened. And I fell. For a dreadful, endless moment the sky was beneath me and the world was far above.

Then my legs slammed into something and I instinctively clung to it with all the strength of my desperation.

Gasping for breath, I blinked. And then it was that I felt fear. Numbing fear ... hopeless fear.

For I had fallen upon the hideous ghastozar, and was now seated astride the most dreadful monster of the skies. . . .

Mad Empress of Callisto

Lin Carter

WILDSIDE PRESS

Mad Empress of Callisto
is dedicated to
Vernell Coriell
of the House of Greystoke
and to the membership of
The Burroughs Bibliophiles.

Contents

Across the Gulf of Space:

An Introduction

The discovery of the Lost City of Arangkhôr in the jungles of southern Cambodia has been hailed as one of the most important archaeological finds in recent history.

The story first broke in the summer of 1969, and the first detailed report appeared in the December 1969 issue of the British periodical *Discovery: The Magazine of Archaeology*. In that issue an article by the journalist Ramsay Edmunds, titled "Mystery City of the Khymer Kings," reported first details of the historic discovery of the age-old, long-forgotten capitol of the mysterious Khymer empire. The leader of the expedition was the famous British archaeologist Sir Malcolm Jerrolds, whose wonderfully exciting book, *Unsolved Mysteries of Asia*, published in 1964 by Macmillan, had predicted just such a discovery.

At the time, the American newspapers were full of the discovery. *Newsweek* quoted Sir Malcolm as hailing the finding of Arangkhôr as "one of the most important archaeological finds since the excavations of Pompeii or Knossos, and ultimately to prove even more significant." The *New York Times* quoted him as saying that the history of Southeast Asia would now have to be rewritten, for a lost chapter of that history was now slowly coming to light.

I doubt if anyone in America was more intensely interested in this exciting discovery than my wife and I, because we were in on the story from the very beginning; in fact, from *before* the beginning. It came about in this manner:

The first man to stumble upon the ruined city was

an American pilot named Jon Dark. Captain Dark was leading a rescue mission to a Vietnamese village hit by Cong terrorists, when his helicopter was forced down across the Cambodian border by engine troubles. In the Lost City—by his own account—he discovered a mysterious prehistoric installation by which he was transported to another planet. This incredible claim has yet to be successfully challenged, or, for that matter, successfully proved factual. But the fact does remain that, utilizing this uncanny "Gateway Between the Worlds," Captain Dark sent back to earth a handwritten manuscript which contained a journal of his adventures and explorations on a world whose peoples called it "Thanator." Addressed to an Air Force buddy, Major Gary Hoyt, who was then stationed in Saigon, the manuscript eventually came into my hands, and I edited it into a typescript and gave it to Dell Books for publication.

Both Dark and Hoyt, it seems, were great fans of American science fiction stories, in particular of the kind of fantastic adventure yarn made popular by Edgar Rice Burroughs, Leigh Brackett, Andre Norton, and myself. Cautiously declining to accept Captain Dark's manuscript as anything more than just an attempt at writing a Burroughs-type novel, Major Hoyt passed the manuscript along to me. He mailed it to my home on Long Island with a covering letter saying I was free to do anything I liked with the "novel"—if, indeed, it *was* only a novel—even to have it published if I thought it was worthy of publication.

The date on which I received the first of what has now proved to be several volumes of Dark's journals is a date forever stamped upon my memory. It was the morning of November 27, 1969. At that time I had only just begun editing the Adult Fantasy Series for Ballantine Books, and I was not as accustomed then to receiving unsolicited manuscripts submitted for my editorial eye as I have since become. Thus, even though the untidy bundle of ramshackle manuscript was handwritten and difficult to make out in places, I gave it much closer attention than I might today, swamped as I now am with submissions.

I found the story marvelously entertaining and exciting and suspenseful—a thoroughly professional attempt at storytelling in the finest tradition of Burroughs' John Carter of Mars books. The adventures of a lone Yank on a distant world he identified as Callisto, one of the larger moons of Jupiter, was indeed worthy of publication. At the time I was engaged in selling some novels and anthologies of my own to Dell Books, because one of my favorite editors, Gail Morrison, had recently changed jobs, moving from Belmont to Dell. I had sold her several novels when she had worked at Belmont, and was delighted to continue our business relationship after she joined the staff of Dell. (For one thing, Dell paid more money.)

Gail was probably too young to have read much Burroughs herself, but she knew his kind of adventure fiction was enormously popular and had, even today, a vast and enthusiastic readership. When I described Dark's book to her as "Burroughsian," she wanted to see it. I prepared a typescript of the novel and submitted it to her *under Dark's name,* listing myself on the title page of the manuscript as editor.

At this she balked, perhaps understandably. I don't think she quite believed my account of having received the manuscript from an unknown author who was still listed then, as he is now, as officially missing in action. She said, quite firmly, that she loved the story and would be proud to publish it, but only if my name appeared on the book as its author. To this I rather reluctantly agreed. But, as I had no desire to pass off the work of another writer as my own, I insisted on adding an introduction to the manuscript, telling exactly how it had come into my hands. Gail made no objection to this, for she knew that Edgar Rice Burroughs had often added a foreword to his own stories, such as the Pellucidar books, pretending to have received the narrative via short-wave radio from the earth's interior, and so on. I guess she thought that I was imitating this tongue-in-cheek Burroughsian trait, even as I was imitating Burroughs' own style in the narrative itself.

The first book was published by Dell in December of 1972 under the title of *Jandar of Callisto.* The delay of almost three years between the acceptance of the manuscript and its eventual publication was caused by the discovery of two more manuscripts, which had to be edited and typed and put into production. The second of these, also published in December 1972, we called *Black Legion of Callisto;* the third, released in January of 1973, was called *Sky Pirates of Callisto.* By the time these books got into print, Gail Morrison was happily married—to my own agent, as it turned out!—and had retired from publishing. Her position at Dell was filled by a young man named David Harris.

In the meantime I had gone to considerable trouble to find out who Jonathan Andrew Dark really was, and how much of his story I could believe. Perhaps I should clearly state here and now that the name I have used in these books, Jonathan Andrew Dark, is *not* his actual name. The real name of the author of these novels is similar in sound, but it is *not* the name I have used. I conceal his actual name to spare the feelings of his relatives, if any, who believe him to be still missing in action. But my contacts in Washington, and officials of the International Red Cross, have confirmed to my satisfaction not only that such a man does exist, that he was lost on a routine helicopter flight as his own account and Gary Hoyt's assure me, but also that he is listed in the official records as being unmarried and without any family.

Acting on information given in the original manuscript of *Jandar of Callisto,* Sir Malcolm Jerrolds in 1969 organized a small expedition into the Mekong Delta region of southeastern Cambodia and, as all the world knows by now, did in fact discover the Lost City exactly where Jandar said it was. Neither Ramsay Edmunds' article about the find, in *Discovery*, nor any of the newspaper accounts of the time contained any reference either to Dark or myself or the book *Jandar of Callisto*, for the very good reason that at the time Jerrolds went into the Cambodian jungles the book not only had yet to be published, it had yet to be accepted by my publisher.

Jerrolds found the city very much as Jandar had described it in the manuscript. He found, also, the mysterious jade-lined "well" that is the earth terminus of the uncanny transporter beam system which Jandar claims connects this planet and Callisto, moon of Jupiter. Although nothing about the well has yet appeared in any of the newspaper accounts of the finding of Arangkhôr, Sir Malcolm in his correspondence with me admits that the peculiar and perhaps synthetic crystalline substance wherewith the well is lined does emit an odd fluorescent effect at certain intervals of time—usually during the hours of night, *and always while the planet Jupiter is above the horizon.* Sir Malcolm, no physicist, believes this to be a residual effect of natural radioactivity.

The success of the three volumes of Captain Dark's journals has in a most satisfying manner justified my own opinion, and that of Gail Morrison, that these stories are, indeed, of professional caliber, and that a large and furiously enthusiastic audience does still exist for adventure stories written in the great Edgar Rice Burroughs tradition.

That is, *Jandar of Callisto* became an overnight sensation on the paperback stands of America, and the entire first printing—of 75,000 copies!—was sold out before the book had been on sale four weeks. In fact, *Jandar* went back to press for a second printing before the month was out. Since then, the second and third volumes of the series have also been reprinted.

Dell's new editor, David Harris, was jubilant the morning he called me on Long Island to report that we had a runaway best seller on our hands.

He was also intensely interested in persuading me to "write" a fourth book as a sequel!

I'm afraid I fobbed him off with the excuse that I was too busy with other work in progress. The fact is that he, like the majority of my readers, rather naturally assumed that my pose of being only the "editor" of these manuscripts was nothing but a good-natured hoax of the same sort as Burroughs' pretense of taking down the Mars Books in shorthand dictated by John Carter himself, who returned to earth at intervals in his astral form to relate his latest adventures to his amanuensis at Tarzana.

But as the sales charts soared and continued to soar, David Harris became increasingly insistent, offering an advance higher than any I have ever received for any novel published under the name of Lin Carter. My dilemma, you perceive, was a peculiar one probably unique in science fiction history.

It was Sir Malcolm Jerrolds, oddly enough, who came to my rescue in the veritable nick of time. Since he first found the Lost City and got in touch with me in order to forward newly received manuscripts, we have exchanged many letters and have become quite good friends. Jerrolds, on more than one occasion, invited my wife and me to visit the "dig" if we ever came to Cambodia. Now, both Noël and I are great archaeology buffs: when she was at college, long before we met and married, my wife caught the virus of enthusiasm, studied Egyptian hieroglyphics, and yearned to become an archaeologist; and I have had a consuming interest in antiquity since first reading, at the impressionable age of twenty-one, C.W. Ceram's magnificent book *Gods, Graves, and Scholars*. So, as you can easily guess, we were afire with excitement at the notion of visiting the Lost City as guests of a genuine archaeological expedition whose fantastic discoveries were making sensational headlines in newspapers around the world.

We were, in fact, studying airline schedules, arranging for passport visas, and making up an itinerary with our travel agents, when fate—or something—

intervened. Prince Sihanouk was deposed while on a
visit to Moscow, the Lon Nol regime was set up,
Communist incursions across the borders touched off a
full-scale revolution, and President Nixon permitted
American troops to enter Cambodia to support the
shaky Phnompenh government. Under such extremely hazardous conditions, the State Department did not
advise U.S. civilians to enter a potentially explosive
trouble spot. So our trip was canceled.

But the situation has since improved considerably.
The State Department still was not enthusiastic
over our plans of visiting Cambodia, but with a bit
of covert assistance from an old friend and science
fiction colleague named David Kyle, who owns a radio station and a piece of a couple of newspapers in
upstate New York, I managed to get myself accredited as a war correspondent, with a temporary press
visa for the Cambodian war zone. I even managed to
have Noël accredited as a photographer, passing ourselves off as a news team.

We were getting ready to leave for Cambodia,
when the big package arrived with the Pnompenh
postmark. Noël was out of the house, having con-
ducted the last contingent of our eight dogs up to the
kennels where they would be housed while we were
out of the country. I was alone in the house, doing
some last-minute packing and addressing some letters and manuscripts to my agent, when the doorbell
rang. It was, of course, the postman with a huge par-
cel from Sir Malcolm.

The thick, crude papyrus sheets and the minute
quill-pen handwriting in the watery, homemade ink
were by now very familiar to me. This time the
uncanny link between two worlds had transported
across the gulf of 387,930,000 miles, not just *one*
booklength manuscript—*but two!*

It was too late to postpone our trip in order to
read and edit the manuscripts; our press visas would
expire before the job could possibly be completed.
But, I realized, I could certainly take the untidy bundle of reed papyrus along with us to read on the

plane, and, when we got back from Cambodia in October, I would be able to edit the typescript for Dell.

However, there was something else I could do!

I went upstairs to the phone outside my study and called Dell Books and asked for my editor, David Harris. It was not yet lunchtime, so I thought I had a good chance of finding him in his office. And I did.

"Hi, Dave? Lin Carter," I said into the receiver. "Fine, thanks. And I've got good news for you. . . ."

The first volume of my "good news" is in your hands right now, and the second volume will soon be ready. They made Dave Harris and Dell Books happy: I hope you enjoy them, as well.

LIN CARTER

Hollis, Long Island, New York

PUBLISHER'S NOTE

This is the fourth volume in Lin Carter's exciting series of novels concerning the adventures of Jandar—a series which Mr. Carter's many enthusiastic readers are already beginning to call "The Callisto Books." The first three books in this exciting new series are *Jandar of Callisto, Black Legion of Callisto,* and *Sky Pirates of Callisto,* which are meant to be read in that order. Now in their second printing, all of the novels in this series are currently in print and should be available from your local paperback stand. If, however, you are unable to find them for any reason, you may order them by writing to Dell Books at the address printed on the reverse of the title page. Happy reading!

—DELL BOOKS

Book One

ZAMARA OF THARKOL

Chapter 1

On the Great Plains

Man's inability to foresee future events is one of Nature's kindest gifts.

Had I but known what would come about from that day's idle hunting expedition, no power in the world could have forced me to stir from the city of my beloved mate.

But a month of festivities and celebrations had begun to pall on one who was more accustomed to peril and adventure than to interminable laudatory speechmaking and the laying of cornerstones. And besides, the *vanth* were migrating.

Once each year this species of game traverses the Great Plains of Haratha to their mating grounds in the valleys of the Black Mountains. You might describe the *vanth* as stag or elk, for they are the closest you can come in terrene equivalents. A large quadruped, hunted for its succulent meat, which is greatly favored by the Shondakorians; a beast, however, not befurred but covered with a slick, supple hide like that of the seal or the dolphin; but a beast whose brow bears up a branching staglike crown of antlers nonetheless.

At any other season of the Thanatorian year, the *vanth* are elusive and fleet-footed game, difficult to catch and hopeless quarry to chase if you happen to be mounted on the restive and unruly *thaptors* the inhabitants of the Jungle Moon employ in lieu of horses. The *thaptor* is a large, feathered but wingless avian vaguely like a cross between the ostrich and the legendary gryphon, and, like the ostrich, capable of attaining remarkable speed. But its gallop, if I

may employ the word, consists of spurts of brief duration, while the mighty *vanth* can run all day without tiring.

During the short migratory season, however, the
vanth traverse the Great Plains in gigantic herds,
their single purpose consisting of the mating urge.
The presence of mounted huntsmen, which at any
other season would disperse them in rapid flight in
all directions, they ignore at this season, intent only
on reaching their mating grounds in the distant
mountains.

Thus, with dawn, a gaily caparisoned hunting
party rode forth from the great gates of the Golden
City of Shondakor to hunt the *vanth*. And thus a se-
quence of events was set into motion which was to
forever alter the destiny of a mighty empire and to
reshape the future history of many nations.

I, Jandar of Callisto, soldier of fortune from the distant planet Earth, and my beloved Princess, Darloona of Shondakor, rode in the forefront of this expedition. Scarce a month before—as we Earthlings
measure the passage of time—had we been wed, upon
the success of my mission to rescue the Princess of the
Ku Thad from her captivity and to destroy for all
time that race of cruel and despotic warriors, the
Sky Pirates of Zanadar. After innumerable adventures
on the mysterious planet of Thanator, or Callisto,
fifth moon of distant Jupiter, I had won a double
victory: the conquest of Zanadar, the City in the
Clouds; and the conquest of the heart of the most
beautiful and desirable woman of two worlds.

Despite the alienage of my birth and despite my
lack of noble or aristocratic lineage, I wed the
woman I loved with the wholehearted consent of
her people and of the peers of her realm. And today
I reigned beside her as Prince of the Golden City.
Such are the traditions of the Ku Thad race: the custom of a prince-consort is unknown to them.

We were very happpy, she and I.

On that fateful morning, as we rode from Shonda-

kor to hunt the mighty *vanth* across the Great
Plains, we were accompanied by a party of our
dearest friends and most loyal courtiers. Among
these was the handsome and dashing Prince Valkar,
with whom I had formed a firm friendship while we
had both served incognito among that bandit-horde
called the Chac Yuul, now long since dispersed and
broken. With us as well rode gallant and chivalrous
Lukor of Ganatol, that master swordsman who had
taught me the ancient and noble science of the blade.

As well, there rode in our company the tall, gaunt,
and solemn-eyed Koja of the Yathoon Horde, an
alien insectoid creature, who had been my first friend
on all of Thanator and into whose cold and passion-
less heart I had instilled the precepts of friendship.
The ugly and doggedly devoted Ergon, a former slave
of the Perushtarians, and the somber but valiant and
heroic Zantor, who had been a great captain among
the Corsairs of the Clouds, rode with us as well. And
in our train thundered a half-company of the guardsmen of Shondakor, armed against any unlikely danger.

Oh, we were a gay and laughing band, as we rode
forth from the Golden City that bright and brilliant morn!

How soon . . . how very soon . . . our gaiety was
to darken with black tragedy and our laughter turn
to grim sorrow . . . and again I say, we mortals are
fortunate that the future remains clouded and unknown, so that we may enjoy each moment to the
full, happily ignorant of what is soon to come.

It was Darloona who first sighted the white *vanth*.
Her glorious eyes flashed with excitement, her lithe
body stretched in the saddle as she spurred her capricious *thaptor* into full gallop. Off she sped, the long
grasses sighing in her wake, one slim arm holding
poised and ready the slender javelin.

Only a half-instant later I flew after her, jolting
my steed into the charge, following the floating banner of her gorgeous scarlet mane. Ere long I had

caught up to her and we rode together, side by side, in pursuit of the *vanth*.

A white *vanth* is exceedingly rare and the hunts-men of Callisto consider such a beast a great prize. And our *vanth* was indeed white as the new-fallen snow—a superb brute, fully grown, bearing up its proud crown of antlers like the unchallenged mon-arch of the wilderness he was.

On ahead of us he fled in great gliding bounds, flying like the wind. We uged our *thaptors* to an even swifter stride, lest the beast escape us by reason of its untiring and superior speed. In no time we had left the rest of our party far behind, with the sole exception of the determined Ergon. His squat, muscu-lar figure bent over the saddlebow, his scarlet face dark with exertion, bald pate gleaming with perspi-ration, the Perushtarian flung himself after us before any of the others could follow.

I turned laughing back at him, aflame with the speed of the chase and the excitement of it all, and he twisted his ugly, square-jawed face from its cus-tomarily sour expression into a gleeful, froglike grin. Immensely strong he was broad-shouldered, deep-chested Ergon, for all his diminutive height and bowed legs. We had been slaves together in the Per-ushtarian city of Narouk, and had fought side-by-side among the gladiators of Zanadar, and the ugly, loyal little man was the most faithful of friends.

On and on ahead of us the white *vanth* bounded, gliding with an almost magical swiftness through the long, sere grasses of the Great Plains of Haratha. Ere long my *thaptor* faltered, gasping for breath through its gaping parrot beak, savage orange eyes rolling wildly. I strove to urge it on, employing the small wooden club called an *olo* which is hung at the saddlebow for precisely that purpose; but it was no good, for my steed was winded and its charge slowed, as did the four-legged bird-horses ridden by Ergon and my beloved. We would lose the *vanth*, we knew, and must return to accept the laughing mock-ery of our fellow hunters with chagrin.

But—no!—for even as our mounts slowed, the *vanth* itself faltered in its flight, and, although it maintained a considerable lead on us, the beast no longer flew before us with the wings of the wind. Perchance it had strained a tendon in its headlong and precipitous flight, for I could see that it limped, gingerly putting its weight on one foreleg.

At any rate, from whatever cause, we still had a chance of coming within javelin-reach of the white *vanth;* so, instead of turning about to rejoin our comrades, now far behind us on the plain, we pressed on in hot pursuit of the limping *vanth* at diminished speed. And played into the hands of Destiny in so doing. . . .

The Great Plains of Haratha are aptly named. From the inland sea of Sanmur Laj in the remote west to the Black Mountains of the far east, they dominate the southern half of this Jungle Moon from the trackless jungles of the Grand Kumala on the equator to the austral pole itself—at least on the one hemisphere of Thanator known to me and to my companions; for the other side of this world, as I have elsewhere stated, yet remains an unexplored and impenetrable region of mystery.

For many hundreds of *korads,* then, the plains stretch, league after league of desolate prairie whose long grasses sigh and whisper beneath the winds. But by no means are the Great Plains of Haratha unbroken flatlands, for here and there, like miniature islands amidst an ocean, small clumps of trees break the monotony of the prairie. Generally, these are *jaruka* trees, which, with their gnarled and knotted black trunks and branches and thick growth of uncanny scarlet foliage, are the most common arboreal flora of the Jungle Moon.

Towards one such stand of trees, our limping quarry now directed his faltering flight, hoping, quite obviously, to evade his hunters amidst the heavily overgrown copse.

As we neared the clump of trees in turn, we could

not help but notice that even as our snow-white quarry was himself an unusual rarity among his kind, so were the trees among which he sought safe refuge.

That is to say, while the common *jaruka* tree has a black trunk and scarlet foliage, the copse ahead of us seemed to be made up of an equally unusual arboreal rarity, the *sorad* tree, which reverses the normal coloration, and boasts jet-black leafage with trunk and branches of curious scarlet wood. This copse in particular, I noted without thinking anything of it at the time, was also unusual in the extreme height of the *sorad* trees whereof it was composed. Commonly, it is yet a third species, the *borath* tree, which attains the greater heights; yet these *sorads*, their massive girth denoting hoary centuries of growth, soared to a stately height such as I have never before seen upon Thanator.

Unerringly did the limping *vanth* make for the safe refuge of this tall stand of *sorad* trees.

Unfalteringly did we direct our winded *thaptors* on its track.

We entered the grove virtually on the heels of the staggering *vanth*, but the underbrush was so thickly grown that neither Ergon nor Darloona nor I could freely cast our light javelins in an attempt to bring it down.

A narrow glade cut into the heart of the copse. Down its length the white *vanth* fled—but it was brought up short at the end of this glade, for here a solid wall of century-old *sorads* rose like a great palisade.

We sprang from our *thaptors* and advanced on foot as the white *vanth* turned at bay to face its hunters.

Darloona's glorious emerald eyes flashed with the excitement of the chase. Her superb bosom rose and fell, pantingly, as she breathed. Poised like a dancing-girl, my Princess confronted the *vanth* with lifted javelin. Against the gloom of the thick woods, the mighty beast glimmered ghostly white.

And then, like the phantom it so resembled, it— *vanished!*

And in its place stood a small, dwarfed figure, swathed in heavy robes of neutral gray.

A strange little man, placid and plump-faced and smiling, with a butter-yellow skin, a bald head, and cold, slitted eyes of gelid ink-black venom.

Darloona gasped at this astounding apparition. Only a moment before the magnificent white *vanth* had turned at bay, menacing us with its crown of antlers.

Now it had melted into this air . . . and, in its place, a dwarfed figure in gray, smiling and enigmatic.

Magic! Or—dream?

Frozen with astonishment, I stood rooted to my tracks, staring at the yellow dwarf.

By my side, burly-chested Ergon glowered, one calloused paw gripping the heft of the great bronze war axe that seldom was far from his side.

"Where did yonder fellow spring from, Jandar?" he growled.

I shrugged. "As well ask, whither vanished the great white *vanth* we followed," I said.

"What *vanth* is that?" He grunted, curiously.

I stared at him, wondering if I had heard correctly.

"The great white *vanth* that fled before us across the plains," I said, wondering if we were both mad.

He looked at me in astonishment.

"I saw no *vanth*," he said puzzledly, "white or otherwise!"

Darloona and I exchanged a stare of amazement.

"But—!" I started to protest. But my protest was never concluded.

Because just then the weighted nets fell upon us from the branches overhead.

Chapter 2

Kidnapped in the Clouds

It was all done so swiftly that it was over within seconds. A mind of consummate cunning, quite obviously, had spun the web which now entrapped us. But it was accomplished with such bewildering swiftness, that, at the time, I was too busy striving to cope with the mere succession of events to think much about it.

The nets were weighted with heavy stones and bore us to the ground. We sprawled, entangled in the meshes, and before either Ergon or I could free ourselves sufficiently to draw the hunting knives we wore scabbarded at our girdles, a horde of red-skinned men fell upon us from the branches above. They had the scarlet skin of Perushtarians, but their heads were covered with long black hair which they wore woven into a single thick queue down the back of the neck, like Chinamen.

This meant that, whatever they were, they were not Perushtarians, or, at least, not Perushtarians of pure-blooded descent. For the red men of the merchant empire were bald as so many eggs.

At the time, of course, I was too busy struggling against the many hands which clutched at me to worry about modes of hirsute adornment. This struggle, of course, was futile: tangled in the web as I was, I could not free my hands in order to cut my way free or use the sword I wore at my shoulder-baldric. Neither could Ergon, for all his burly strength. Our adversaries were too many in sheer weight of number, and had planned and doubtlessly rehearsed their attack in such wise as to render us helpless and securely trussed in half a minute.

We were disarmed, our wrists securely bound behind our backs with rawhide thongs, gags thrust into our mouths, and it was all accomplished with dazzling speed of execution. Then the squat red men with the thick black queues of plaited hair cut us free of the nets and dragged us to our feet, propelling us across the clearing and into the depths of the woods.

And all this while the yellow dwarf stood watching, a cold gloating smile crinkling his cold black slitted eyes.

In a detached manner, I could not help feeling an abstract sort of admiration for the speed and timing and efficiency with which our capture was accomplished. We were not handled with any particular brutality; neither were any indignities used against my Princess, although she was furious and raging, as was I. At the time, I did not feel any singular fear. Our captors had immobilized and disarmed us with great skill and cunning, but I remained calm and unworried, although I desired nothing more than to be free of my bonds and to get a sword into my hands.

The dispassion wherewith I viewed our present plight may easily be explained. I viewed our predicament, you see, as a temporary one. Not ten minutes behind us rode our true and loyal friends, Luker, Valkar, and Zantor. The master swordsman of Ganatol, the heroic son of Lord Yarrak, and the mightiest champion of the gladiators of Zanadar would be upon the scene in minutes at the most, and against their blades the squat, red-skinned ambushers would be helpless, for all their number. And at the heels of our friends rode a half-company of armed Shondakorian guardsmen.

No—thought I, detachedly—we had nothing to fear. Our position, although humiliating and uncomfortable, was temporary at most. Rescue, freedom, and vengeance rode towards us through the grassy plains with the speed of the wind.

Or so I thought at the time.

Our captors hurried us along through the thick underbrush and then thrust us into the most peculiar contraption.

It was like nothing more than an immense wicker
basket woven of tough river reeds and stiffened with
ribs of a light, fibrous, hollow, and tubular wood that
resembled bamboo in all respects save that of coloration.

This basket was large enough to hold fifteen persons, as was shortly proved. For the dozen or so men
who had seized us, together with the yellow, slant-
eyed dwarf in neutral gray, and a young woman of
aristocratic and even imperious bearing and hauteur
joined us within the inexplicable enclosure.

I had naturally expected to be bundled into the
saddle of a *thaptor,* for how else could our kidnap-
pers hope to bear us away from swift and certain rescue? But the immense basket sat on the thickly grassed
ground. It proved not even to be a wickerwork
chariot as I had thought it to be at first glance. No,
the huge light thing of woven reeds was hung from
the branches above, for long woven cables or ropes
went up from the rim of the basket into the leafy
gloom above our heads.

What in the world did our captors hope to accom-
plish by this inexplicable act? I exchanged a wide-
eyed glance and eloquent shrug with Ergon and Darloona. Were we in the hands of a pack of raving
madmen? Did they hope to hide thus from the gaze
of our rescuers? That was absurd and ludicrous: Valkar
and the others would comb every square inch of this
stand of trees until they found us.

As yet not one of our captors had so much as uttered a single word.

Now the imperious young woman who had joined
us in the basket delivered a command in a sharp,
clear voice.

"Cut us free, Zapur!"

One of the warriors plucked a hooked knife from
his girdle, leaned from the basket, and began to saw
at yet another rope. This rope was tied about the

lower trunk of the nearer of the *sorad* trees. Simultaneously, another warrior leaned out from the other side of the basket and began cutting through a second rope, secured about another *sorad* trunk on the other side.

Surely, our captors were deranged! Their actions simply made no sense. And yet, with what cunning and sense of timing the red men had planned and carried out their plot! A cold little wind of intuition blew against the back of my neck.

A moment later, my intuition proved valid.

Our captors were not insane. Indeed, they knew exactly what they were doing.

For we jerked loose from the ground and swung up into the air!

Ergon and Darloona were struck wide-eyed with amazement. What was happening seemed to them inexplicable and utterly astonishing. I, too, was astonished; but I alone understood what was happening . . . and my former confidence at the certainty of a swift and easy rescue emptied from me on the moment, to be replaced by a growing fear . . .

For, while I had thought the only aerial transport known to the denizens of Callisto to be the flying ships of the Zanadarian pirates, this type of lighter-than-air craft had been used on my native Earth for generations before I had been born.

In short—*we were riding in a balloon!*

The capacious wickerwork basket was suspended by woven cables from a huge air tight gasbag filled, I suppose, either with heated air or with some gas akin to hydrogen or helium. The balloon itself was of some shiny woven material like oiled silk or wax-impregnated linen. Painted black, it had been invisible to us in the darkness of the copse, hidden among the black foliage of the *sorad* trees. Once cut loose, it swung aloft in instants. Now we cleared the topmost branches of the tall trees and floated free on the winds of the upper air.

The clump of trees dwindled beneath us. At the

very edge of the copse I saw some of our would-be rescuers riding into the woods. Of course, it never occurred to any of our friends to look up and to search
for us in the clouds!

I understood now why we had been so tightly and
thoroughly gagged. And, remembering my former
aloof amusement at our pointless captivity, and my
bland assumption that rescue and vengeance lay only
minutes away, I felt the sickening impact of worry,
as the grim realization of how desperate our situation actually was came home to me.

But there was nothing I could do about it . . . at
least for the present.

The young woman was laughing in delight and excitement at the success of the coup. Triumph flashed
in her eyes as she exchanged a few words with the
yellow dwarf, then glanced over at me with amusement. I eyed her grimly, inwardly furious.

She was a curious figure, I realized. Young and very
beautiful, with the red skin of a Perushtarian. But,
like the others, she was no Perushtarian, for the long
silken banner of her glistening black hair floated on
the winds about us. She wore an odd gown in a style
unfamiliar to me, a light garment of silken stuff,
tightly stretched across her breasts and fastened
with a jeweled brooch over one shoulder, leaving the
other shoulder and arm bare. She was, quite evi-
dently, a woman of considerable wealth and importance, for expensive gems flashed at throat and ear,
rings of precious metal adorned her slender hands,
and a coronet of odd design encircled her brows,
flashing with precious stones.

But I had not the slightest notion of who she was.
To the very best of my memory, I had never laid
eyes on her before in all my life, and I had no idea of
why she had kidnapped us.

It was very obvious that the young woman was in
command of this situation. The stolid-faced, bow-
legged red warriors deferred to her with every token
of awe and subservience. Even the little yellow dwarf
with the slitted black gaze seemed in her service. She

stood, tall, lithe, and laughing, one jeweled hand clinging to the guide ropes of the balloon, imperious and triumphant as a queen.

But queen of *what*—and *where?*

Few and widely-separated are the cities of Thanator the Jungle Moon. Several of the civilizations that share this world between them are wandering and homeless nomad peoples, like the insectoids of the Yathoon Horde or the bandits of the now-disbanded Chac Yuul legion. Our only enemies, the Sky Pirates of Zanadar, we had but recently destroyed, laying their city in ruins. And they dwell in the White Mountains, far away to the northwest. The red empire of the Perushtarians is situated many *korads* to the northeast of Shondakor; and the four Perushtarian cities of Farz, Narouk, Soraba, and imperial Perusht itself, are widely scattered about the shores of the landlocked sea of Corund Laj. The nearest of the seven cities of Thanator to golden Shondakor is the city of Tharkol, which stands amidst the equatorial plains in the eastern extremity of the hemisphere.

With none of these seven cities is Shondakor currently at enmity, much less at war. With the exception of the Perushtarian merchant empire, the cities of Callisto are lone and individual sovereignties. Our relations with the city-states of Ganatol or Tharkol, for instance, are few; we exchange no ambassadors and we indulge in no trade or commerce. Both cities are vastly inferior to golden Shondakor in size, wealth, or power. For either metropolis to contemplate war with the Golden City of the Ku Thad would be absurd. They would have nothing to gain and everything to lose, for, having but recently broken the power of the Chac Yuul bandit legion, and having for all time exterminated the aerial corsairs of distant Zanadar, we have in recent months emerged as the most powerful nation on this planet.

Only the red empire of the Perushtarians are more numerous than the Ku Thad in terms of populace,

and more wealthy. But the red men of Perushtar are
the least warlike of all the nations of Thanator.
They are a nation of tradesmen, a mercantile civilization like that of the ancient Carthaginians in the
remote history of my own world.

For them to challenge the might of victorious
Shondakor would be folly and madness. They do not
even maintain a standing army, and during the long
recent decades during which their trading caravans
and merchant fleets were preyed upon by the flying
corsairs of Zanadar, they grudgingly paid an annual
tribute to assure their immunity from the depreda-
tions of the Sky Pirates, rather than raise an army
of war.

Bound and gagged and helpless to discuss the situation with my Princess or Ergon, I could only lie,
seething with silent rage, while these questions
boiled through my turbulent thoughts.

By this time we had ascended to the height of at
least half a mile into the air, and were drifting due
east on the prevailing winds. Or so I guessed, anyway. It is somewhat difficult to judge one's direction
on Callisto. The inhabitants of the Jungle Moon
have yet to invent the compass, and as this world is
illuminated by a layer of luminous golden vapor in its
atmosphere, one never sees the sun and thus cannot
with ease or surety judge east from west, which is
the easiest thing to do on my own native Earth. But
judging the direction of our flight as best I could, we
were flying east . . . east, towards the unknown edge
of the world itself, for, as I have said, the far side of
Callisto is a realm of unexplored mystery to the na-
tives of this planet. Nothing at all is known of the
other hemisphere, save that somewhere therein re-
sides a mysterious people called the Mind Wizards of
Kuur, with whom I have already had one encounter.

As related in an earlier volume of these memoirs*,
while serving incognito among the warriors of the

---

* A book entitled *Black Legion of Callisto,* published by Dell
Books in December 1972.

Chac Yuul, I discovered that one of the advisors of Arkola, chief of the Black Legion, was a Kuurian named Ool the Uncanny. A little plump, placid Buddha of a man, bald, with slitted eyes and butter-yellow skin, the clever and cunning little priest had been none other than the power behind the throne, so to speak. A shudder ran through me at the memory of that uncanny battle in the Pits, when I had crossed swords with the cunning Ool, in a desperate, last-minute attempt to rescue my beloved Princess from a forced marriage with Prince Vaspian, the son of Arkola the Usurper. Although I am in my own right a master swordsman, Ool proved almost my match, for the little Kuurian possessed the weird power of mental telepathy and thus could read my mind and know my every thought. It is, as I discovered during that desperate duel in the dungeons, almost impossible to conquer a swordsman who can read your mind . . .

Suddenly I stiffened where I lay, helplessly bound in the basket of the drifting balloon!

Ool had been a little man, almost a dwarf . . . yellow-skinned and bald, with slanted eyes, gowned in a priestlike robe of gray . . .

My gaze flashed across the crowded basket to where the yellow dwarf squatted. His clever and beady black eyes bored into mine, almost knowingly. Almost as if he knew or guessed the direction of my thoughts, a cold and crafty smile hovered about his thin lips—*and he nodded.*

I tore my gaze from his slanted eyes, and lay stunned in realization.

One of the many mysteries that surrounded our capture was now solved.

For the malignant, gloating little dwarf, with butter-yellow skin *was a Mind Wizard of distant and unknown Kuur.*

Chapter 3

Prisoners of Tharkol

All the remainder of that long day we flew on, riding the winds far above the Great Plains, on and on
into the remote east.

Our captors loosened our bonds, restoring circula-
tion, and made us comfortable enough. They did not,
however, remove the gags from our mouths for some
reason. We suffered considerably from thirst, therefore.

Time and again I surreptitiously tested my
strength against the rawhide thongs that bound my
arms behind my back. Had I been bound with ropes,
it is just possible that I might have been able to
burst free of them, for, raised under the slightly
heavier gravitational influence of Earth, my strength
is somewhat greater than that of the average
Thanatorian. But rawhide is a devilishly difficult
thing to free oneself of, for as the untanned leather
dries it also shrinks, and, being flexible to a degree,
it "gives" ever so slightly to your efforts to free yourself, instead of breaking.

Thus my attempts were in vain; but still I strove
to loosen my hands. There was nothing else to be
done, and it is not the way of Jandar of Callisto to
yield supinely to captivity or to superior force. Far
rather would I go down fighting with the last ounce
of strength in my body, than to lie helpless without
trying, however hopelessly, to win freedom.

Ergon, too, strove to win free of the thongs. The
burly, sullen-faced warrior was gagged as were I and
Darloona, but his scowling glare was eloquent. Had
his mouth been ungagged, he would have made the

air sulphurous with oaths. From time to time, I saw his scarlet face congested with effort and the great thews that bulged in shoulder and upper arm tense and stand out in sharp relief like steel bands. But his strength, like my own, was insufficient to break free of bondage.

We were still riding the winds when night fell across the world. Nightfall on Callisto comes without warning and the transition from full daylight to ebon gloom takes only minutes. Thus, when the world darkened suddenly around us and the great moons rose, rich with their many colors, we realized we had been in flight for several hours.

Our flight ended shortly after the coming of the darkness. By the green and red and silvery illumination afforded by three of the many moons of Jupiter, we observed a city on the horizon. It rose from a hilly height amidst the plain and was nowhere near the sea, and therefore we assumed that it was none other than Tharkol.

We could not see very much of it because of our position in the basket, but from what we could observe, it was a large city of stone masonry, ringed about with the mighty bastions of a great wall. From a citadel-crowned and heavily fortified hill in the center of the city, broad paved avenues ran in every direction like spokes from the hub of a wheel. Towards this central citadel the queenly young woman guided our aerial vehicle.

The walls of the citadel drifted past below us. By the green rays of Orovad, or Io, which was then at the zenith, we saw beneath us a broad plaza or forum paved with smooth stone. Over this square, which was the courtyard of the citadel, our captress piloted the balloon.

A second ring of fortifications passed beneath us, and then, as the crimson rays of Ganymede added their illumination to the light of the first moon, we saw that the citadel which crowned the hilly height was built like an enormous ziggurat with many tiers.

Towards the third of these tiers we floated, de-

scending as lightly as a floating leaf. Ranks of guardsmen stood stiffly at attention, the green and red
moonlight sparkling from rows of helmets, breast-
plates, and spear blades. At a curt command they
sprang forward, caught the drifting lines and hauled
the basket down, tethering it securely to a lengthy
mast or spar that struck out at an angle from the lip
of the tier and which had obviously been designed
for exactly this purpose.

It was the young woman who was the first to step
from the basket. As she appeared to their view, the
moonlight flashing on the jewels of her coronet, the
ranked guards struck their mailed gauntlets to their
armored breasts in a crashing salute, and thundered
forth a great cry as if from a single throat.

"*Hail, Zamara!*"

So, at least, we had learned the name of our captress.

The guards bundled us out of the basket and lifted
us down to the stone surface of the ziggurat tier, and
again I could not help noticing that we were handled without roughness or insult. Zamara turned,
made an imperious gesture, flashing in my direction
one last triumphant, joyous glance of mockery and
amusement from her brilliant eyes. Then we were
bundled swiftly away, through a doorway whose lin-
tel was carved with beaked and leering mythological
monsters, and through a bewildering maze of cor-
ridors and passages into the citadel itself.

And thus ended our flight across the Great Plains
of Haratha. If captivity must be our lot, at least ours
was luxurious. I had expected to be thrust into the
Pits, to be bedded on verminous and moldy straw in
some lightless and fetid dungeon cell.

Instead, we were imprisoned in one of the upper
levels of the citadel in surroundings of silken and vo-
luptuous comfort. Our "prison cell" was a spacious and
airy apartment, stone walls draped with splendid tapestries, nests of velvet cushions arranged between
low couches covered with rare furs. Few palaces, in
my experience, can boast a more luxurious and beauti-
fully appointed suite for their guests!

Herein, at long last, we were unbound and ungagged. Both Ergon and I had been on the alert for
the moment, and when it came we fully intended to
hurl ourselves on our captors in a desperate bid for
freedom. But in this detail, too, the clever and cunning brain that lay behind the plot had already en-
visioned and forestalled such an attempt on our part.
For as we were untied, alert and vigilant guards
stood about us, many blades held unwaveringly at our
breasts, quite effectively holding us at bay.

Once we were free, and stood glowering at the
guards, helpless to attack, chafing our numb wrists,
the guards backed slowly through the portal and left
us to our own devices. The door, of course, was a
thick and massive slab of the hardest of woods,
bound with bronze studs, and securely locked and
barred from without.

"It seems we are not to be starved, at any rate,"
Ergon grunted sourly. I followed his gesture, to see
low taborets of inlaid wood laden with platters of
cold sliced meat, fresh fruit, cubes of delicious cheese,
and crystal pitchers of golden wine.

Having been gagged for many hours, it was our
thirst which chiefly tormented us. The wine was deliciously cold, of exquisite bouquet and superb vintage.
Once our raging thirst had been assuaged, we became
aware of a ravenous hunger within, and fell to the
other viands with a will. The meats were tender
and delicately spiced, and the fruits and pastries
were richly satisfying.

"How odd of our enemies to imprison us in surroundings of such luxury," Darloona murmured,
glancing about at the gorgeous furnishings. My heart
swelled within me at the calm insouciance of her
tones. Few of her sex could have endured attack, capture, and imprisonment without giving way to an hys-
teria of terror or a storm of tears. But the brave and
gallant Princess of the Ku Thad shrugged off the
indignity of capture and the dread of the unknown
fate reserved for us with the unshaken courage I could
only admire.

For the ten-thousandth time I pondered the mira-

cle of fate that had won me the love of so magnificent a woman!

"Perushtarians," I commented around a mouthful of
fruit, "have a natural love of luxury which extends, it
would seem, even to the decor of their prisons."

It was a feeble jest, God knows, but she laughed
wholeheartedly.

"No Perushtarians these," grunted Ergon glumly.
"You must have have noticed their braided hair, Jandar."

I nodded. "But they have the scarlet skins . . ."

"I am a full-blooded Perushtarian," he pointed out
grimly, "and it is known that something in our
blood inclines us to baldness. There is doubtless a
strain of Perushtarian lineage in these dogs, but another race is blended therein as well. Noticed you
their bandy legs and lankness of hair? What think
you, then?"

Darloona set down her wine goblet with a decisive
click.

"The Black Legion!" she said.

He nodded glumly. "Aye, Lady! And I know of but
one people in whose blood is blended that of the
Chac Yuul and of the Empire as well. *The city of
Tharkol!*"

I rubbed my jaw thoughtfully. "I had assumed as
much myself, Ergon, having noted the general direction of our flight as best I could from the bottom of
that accursed basket. My Princess, has our city been
at enmity with the Tharkolians within your memory?"

She shook her head puzzledly, glorious scarlet mane
curling over bare shoulders.

"We have had naught, or very little, to do with
Tharkol in my reign," she murmured. "And in the
time of my royal father, little enough, beyond occa-
sional trading. The Tharkolians are an unfriendly
people and keep to themselves, for aught I know.
The many long leagues of grassy plain that lie between our cities have, till now, served as a barrier between us."

"It would seem, then, that they have attacked us without provocation," I said.

Her emerald eyes flashed and her superb bosom heaved.

"They shall find they have seized a very *deltagar* by the tail, then, the fools!" she snapped venomously, naming a ferocious jungle predator feared across the breadth of Thanator for its fighting fury.

"By noon tomorrow, I doubt me not, they shall find the unconquerable legions of Shondakor camped before their gates!" she cried.

"I hope you are correct in that, my Princess," I returned quietly. "But I fear me you are not. . . ."

"What mean you, Jandar?" she flashed. "Valkar will waste not a moment in following us thither. To raise the legions of the Ku Thad and to mount an invasion of the lands about Tharkol will be pressed with all speed. Ere long the city will be ringed about with our armies, and I doubt me not but that the hosts of Shondakor will make short work of any such resistance as the Tharkolians may attempt. True, the walls of the city seem stout enough, but recall, my Prince, the two flying galleons at our command: by their employment, a host of valiant Shondakorian warriors may easily be carried over the walls of this accursed city, to invest with ease the very citadel of Queen Zamara . . ."

My beloved was right enough in what she said. The destruction of the City in the Clouds had left us in possession of two of the remarkable aerial warships of the Sky Pirates. These two ornithopters, as the ingenious Zanadarian contrivances are more properly termed, are the *Jalathadar*, captained by Lord Haakon, a gallant Shondakorian of noble birth who had sailed with the *Jalathadar* on her heroic maiden voyage against Zanadar*, and her sister ship, the former corsair vessel, *Xaxar*, which was under the captaincy of her original master, Zantor. We had at

* As related in the novel *Sky Pirates of Callisto*, published by Dell Books in January 1973.

this time no particular reason to doubt that the twin sky-ships were the last of their kind aloft. For, while doubtless several if not many of the Zanadarian warships had been absent from the City in the Clouds at the time of our attack on the pirate stronghold and its destruction, the only known source of the levitating gas which permitted the aerial conveyances to resist the gravity of Thanator had been destroyed in the conflagration which had reduced to ashes the city of the Sky Pirates itself. Lacking the means whereby to recharge their hollow hulls and airtight holds with new supplies of the lifting vapor, most if not all of the flying ships by now were doubtless grounded—a fate which would in time render the *Jalathadar* and the *Xaxar* unable to navigate the skies of Callisto, as well.

I forbore to press the point, deciding it was better to permit my beloved to retain her hopes of early freedom. Nothing was to be gained by sharing with her the reasoning which impelled me to doubt that our rescue by our friends was as imminent as she believed.

But Ergon sensed my reticence. And later, after Darloona retired to her couch, worn out from the excitement of this unexpectedly adventurous day, he sought me where I stood at the barred window, thoughtfully looking out over the vista of the streets and rooftops of Tharkol, bathed in the multicolored light of the many moons.

"Jandar," the ugly, faithful Perushtarian growled in my ear, "you had another reason for doubting the legions of Shondakor would be so quick on our trail, did you not?"

"I did, old friend," I replied somberly.

"May I know it, then?"

I nodded a bit dispiritedly.

"There is no reason why you should not share my inward trepidations, Ergon, although I have good cause to spare my Princess. My reasoning is simple. Valkar will not be able to follow us, because he can have no notion of how we vanished from the copse."

Ergon blinked at me, his heavy visage grim and thoughtful.

"You mean—"

"I mean that the balloon was released even as the guardsmen entered the wood behind us," I said in low tones. "Valkar and the others would have first combed the copse itself, to ascertain that we were not hidden somewhere in the thick underbrush. By the time they made certain of that, and began to scour the countryside for some sign of us, the balloon would have been well out of sight. And besides . . ." I hesitated.

"Yes?" he urged.

I released a weary sigh.

"And besides, Shondakorians know nothing of balloons, which are otherwise unknown across the breadth of Thanator. *And there is simply no reason at all for our friends to have looked for us in the skies. . . ."*

Chapter 4

The Empress of Callisto

With dawn the next day my Princess rose rested and
refreshed, and filled with zest and good humor. It
did not in the slightest serve to dampen her spirits
to discover that the mailed legions of the Golden
City were not as yet encamped about the walls of
Tharkol. Doubtless, she said cheerfully, the host had
ridden through the better part of the night, and
would arrive later in the morning.

Ergon and I exchanged an eloquent glance, but neither of us disabused Darloona of her groundless op-
timism that rescue and vengeance were almost at
hand. Indeed, we strove to put a cheerful face on
events ourselves, in order to protect her peace of
mind. I don't know about Ergon, but, for my part,
this was not easy to do; I had spent a perfectly
wretched night, tossing and turning, unable to quiet
my seething brain until the early hours of morn, in
which exhaustion finally induced an uneasy slumber
shot through with menacing and unpleasant dreams.

We bathed and breakfasted sumptuously. Again I
puzzled—not only as to why the Queen of this city
had caused us to be taken prisoner at all—which
doubtless we would discover in time—but also as to
the peculiar luxury of our imprisonment. Few prisoners are jailed in silken apartments of decor so sumptuous as to befit the housing of state guests of royal
blood.

The answer to this minor mystery, too, we would
doubtless learn in time, I grimly conjectured.

We had just completed our leisurely meal when the
measured tramp of booted feet in the hallway

beyond signaled the arrival of guards come to escort us into the presence of the Queen of Tharkol. It seemed that we should soon learn the answer to at least one of the questions which had plagued me— that is, the reason why the Tharkolians had captured us, thus deliberately performing an act of war against a neighboring kingdom with whom they were, ostensibly at least, at peace.

There was no slightest opportunity afforded us for an attempt at escape. The cortege of guards sent to escort us thither numbered, as I recall, about twenty. The number had been calculated to a nicety, I thought. Had they been any fewer, two determined and desperate warriors, such as Ergon and I, might perchance have risked all on a try for freedom. But *twenty* fully armed warriors . . . the number was too great; to try for a break would have been utter folly, and quite futile.

Thus the guards formed a hollow square, with Darloona and Ergon and I in the center of the square, and marched us through the sumptuous palace of Tharkol and into the throne room of the Queen without a chance of a fight.

The moment we entered the throne room I stopped short in amazement. And perhaps I should explain at this point in my narrative something of the manner in which princes hold state on the Jungle Moon. It has been my experience that the monarchs who rule the city-states of Callisto generally hold court in a large pillared and domed chamber or central hall of their palaces. During such occasions these monarchs are enthroned in a great chair, often situated on a low dais in the center of the hall, a dais usually raised two or three steps higher than the floor of the throne room itself.

Zamara of Tharkol, however, ruled in a different wise!

For one thing, her throne room was the most enormous single room I have ever been in during my entire life. The great hall must have measured no fewer than five hundred feet from wall to wall. It

was an enormous circular space, or rotunda, ringed
with a circle of marble pillars of immense height and
tremendous girth which soared up far above our heads
to support a colossal dome so huge it would have
done credit to the palace of the mightiest emperor.

Around the walls of this enormous rotunda stood,
motionless and in complete silence, a vast throng of
nobles and officials and courtiers. These numbered at
least three times the number of such officials as generally attended a gathering of the court in my own
city of Shondakor. They were Perushtarians, one and
all, with scarlet skins and brilliant black eyes, at-
tired in superb and costly garments which scintil-
lated with colored fabrics and flashed with precious
metals and sparkled with masses of expensive jewel-
ry. The overall effect was stupendous—stunning!

Holding this motionless and unspeaking crowd
back, as it were, a ring of guardsmen stood three
deep, entirely encircling the vast echoing room. Daylight glittered blindingly from polished helm, golden
cuirass, kite shield, and spear blade. Cloaks of black
and scarlet velvet and tall plumes of those same
colors adorned these guards, who were, without exception, men of extraordinary height, physical development, and handsomeness. Like so many Adon-
ises in gold, scarlet, and black, the triple ring of
guards stood, frozen at attention, immobile as
bronze statues. Not one of them was an inch less
than six feet tall.

Again, the cumulative effect was staggering.

At the center of the gigantic hall, Zamara sat enthroned.

Her throne was a ponderous and shimmering thing
of solid electrum which must have weighed a ton or
more. Even if the tremendous throne was only plated
with the precious stuff, the amount of gold and silver
that had gone into the making of the alloy represented in itself the ransom of an imperial province.

And, where most of the Princes of Thanator sit in
state atop a dais consisting of two or three steps,
such proportions were too modest for the likes of

Zamara of Tharkol. *Her* dais was seventeen steps high, and towered above the heads of the throng like a miniature hill!

Her costume consisted entirely of jewels. These were either white or ice-blue diamonds, for the most part, or at least the Callistan equivalent of the diamond, a gem which the races of Thanator name *ramazond.* The wealth of many kingdoms adorned the body of this young woman.

She was certainly one of the most beautiful creatures I have ever set eyes upon. Slim as a sapling, graceful as a dancer, lithe, supple, and dangerous as a leopard, the warm scarlet of her naked arms, long legs, and slim waist contrasted startlingly with the bejeweled treasure she wore. Her face was heart-shaped, vital, alive, with enormous and brilliant eyes and a flowing mane of silken black, caught in a jeweled coronet of flashing stones. She sat in the mighty throne, a vision of incredible wealth, dazzling beauty, and awesome power.

I think I gasped at the sight of her. Directly above her soared the immense dome of lucent crystal. Daylight poured down upon her in a flood of golden fire that struck to glory the magnificent gems which adorned her half-naked body. She was stunning . . . and she knew it!

In that moment of deafening silence when we stood, all three of us, frozen in amazement at the magnificence of this spectacle, an imposing chamberlain rang his mace against the marble pave with a crash of thunder.

"Kneel ye in the presence of Zamara the Magnificent, supreme and unchallenged Empress of all Callisto!" he boomed out in a deep, rolling voice.

As a field of wheat bends all at once beneath the unseen pressure of a mighty wind, so did all that vast throng of courtiers fall to their knees before the tall throne. Only we three captives remained standing.

Zamara caught our astonished gaze across the vast and glittering hall, and smiled a sly and mocking smile.

"The Prince and Princess of Shondakor and their servant may advance to kiss the feet of their Empress," she called sweetly.

Ergon growled deep in his barrel chest, but whether it was from the affront of being called our servant, or from the insult to Darloona and myself, I do not know. As for myself, my fists balled and my jaw settled truculently.

Darloona, however, reacted splendidly. She was royalty born, whereas I was but royalty by marriage, if you know what I mean. She drew herself up splendidly, and made no reply. But the contempt she did not express in words was eloquent in every line of her body.

She was superb! Again I was grateful to the fate that had earned me the love of such a woman.

After a moment of eloquent silence, she spoke. The calm tone of her voice and the serenity of her expression belied the fury that must have seethed and roiled within her breast.

"The Princess of Shondakor will be pleased to extend the hand of friendship to the Princess of Tharkol," she said tranquilly, "in the name of the bonds of mutual respect that have always existed between our cities . . . and of the peace between them which has, heretofore, remained unbroken for a thousand years."

The rebuff was exquisitely delivered. Zamara flushed a deeper crimson and bit her lower lip in vexation as a gasp of startled shock went murmuring through the vast and echoing hall. Doubtless Zamara had thought to shame or fluster my beloved in contrast between their persons—Zamara enthroned in a glamour of incredible magnificence, at the height of her imperial power—and Darloona disheveled, in rude hunting costume, her glorious mane tousled and uncombed, her regalia left behind. But such did not occur. The innate majesty and queenliness of my beloved put to shame the ostentation flaunted by the bejeweled, self-styled "empress." And—what made it all the worse for Zamara—she knew it. And so did everyone else in the room.

We were returned to our apartment and spent the remainder of that day in seclusion. Despite her small victory over Zamara, my Princess was in a perfect fury at this outrage, and paced the length of the room like a caged tigress, boiling with rage. Ergon and I sat together conversing in low tones, discussing our present predicament and our chances of somehow getting out of it.

Although she said nothing about it, I think Darloona knew by now that the host of Shondakor was not going to arrive before the walls of Tharkol in an hour or two, or even a week or two. The very real danger into which chance had thrust us had dawned upon her at last, as it had long since dawned upon Ergon and myself. Darloona's royal fury at the outrage kept her, for the moment, too busy to think out the implications of our imprisonment. But Ergon and I knew them well.

For even if Darloona's uncle, Lord Yarrak, did in fact discover our whereabouts and march to lay siege to Tharkol with the host of the Golden City, it would be stalemate. Zamara would display us on the walls and threaten to have us tortured to death before the entire army of Shondakor unless it surrendered—and, I very much feared, it would surrender. The person and safety of the Warrior Princess was sacred to the Ku Thad, and Zamara of Tharkol knew it well.

But there was another element in our predicament that tormented me. And that was the character of Zamara herself. We were prisoners, completely at the mercy of a megalomaniac who, drunk with pomp, pride, and power, had somehow managed to convince herself that she was destined to dominate the entire planet, and did not hesitate to entitle herself Empress of Thanator.

In a word—she was *mad.*

And there is simply no arguing with an insanc person . . . especially if you happen to be helplessly in her power.

There was no telling what she might do. Because, in her madness, folly, and blind egoism, she was literally capable of doing—*anything!*

Hence it was imperative that we make our escape at once . . .

I have to laugh, looking back on it all. How many times have I read in fantastic fiction of a hero in a similar predicament to that in which Darloona and Ergon and I now found ourselves. Edgar Rice Burroughs, in his wonderful Mars Books, has thrust the valiant John Carter into the clutches of a Barsoomian jeddak a thousand times (indeed, I can't remember a single one of his marvelously entertaining novels in which the hero is not made somebody's prisoner at least *once* in the course of the narrative!), and the ingenuity of the various means whereby the greatest swordsman of two worlds escapes from whatever durance vile he finds himself in has never failed to amuse and entertain me.

But in real life, I am sorry to say, things are very different.

Our cell, though sumptuous, was still a cell—a chamber walled with solid stone, against which the strength of fifty men would exhaust itself without effect. The windows gave forth on a tantalizing vista of wall, street, and rooftops—but were heavily and securely barred with grilles of dense metal, impervious to anything lesser than a battering ram. At least a dozen guards were posted at the only entrance to our suite during every moment of the night and day, and even were I armed and free, it would take a superman to hew a path through so many mailed and vigilant warriors.

No, we were captives, and bound to remain so for the immediate future!

Worn out with futile plans and schemes, we listlessly nibbled at the platters of exquisite viands set out for us, and one by one went to our couches to seek such rest as weary minds might find.

It was several hours later when I came suddenly awake. The room was drowned in darkness, but the window was a tall rectangle of lucent silver lit by the gorgeous orb of Ramavad.

I could not at once think what it was that had so suddenly awakened me. But awake I was, quivering and tense and alert, as if, for all the depth of my exhausted slumbers, some unsleeping faculty had remained on watch, and had roused me as it sensed the stealthy approach of some unseen danger.

There it was again—that furtive ghost of sound!

The slither of sandal leather on naked stone.

And then I froze, every sense thrumming, as if suddenly a gout of ice water had sluiced me from head to foot.

For a man was standing near the head of my couch—I could see the outline of his black-cloaked figure etched in luminous silver from the moonlight streaming through the window—and it was neither Ergon nor Darloona.

Some unknown and mysterious stranger had made his silent, stealthy way into the room by dark of night, and crept towards me in the gloom.

I sprang from my couch and was upon him in a single bound.

And in the very next instant, I was fighting for my life!

Book Two

GLYPTO THE CHANTHAN

Chapter 5

A Secret Passage

Even as I pounced upon the cloaked figure it writhed from my grip. And in the next instant a wicked, hooked little knife flashed at my throat. I blocked the thrust with my forearm, seized the wrist of the assassin's knife hand, and wrung it cruelly, forcing a squeal of pain from the lips of my opponent.

The hooked knife fell on the silken carpets, but my mysterious opponent had yet other weapons. One of these, a bony knee, caught me in the pit of the stomach with sickening force. The breath whooshed from my lungs and I reeled groggily for a moment, struggling to catch my breath.

My opponent seized his opportunity and twisted from my grip. He was as hard to hold onto as a slippery eel, that fellow! In a swirl of his black cape he melted into the shadows of the chamber and had all but vanished as swiftly and mysteriously as he had entered it.

And this, no doubt, he would have done, had it not been for Ergon. We all slept in the same room, you see, but it was a large and capacious chamber with silk-draped couches scattered about, which afforded us considerable privacy. My Princess slept in a couch we had drawn into a niche of the wall, and, for her greater privacy, Ergon and I had rigged up a curtain which veiled the alcove. But Ergon sprawled on a couch across the room from me, snoring lustily.

The muffled sounds of the struggle had roused the faithful fellow. And, even as my slippery adversary wriggled free of my grasp and slunk into the deeper gloom, the burly Perushtarian was upon him with a tigerish lunge. He dealt the cloaked figure a stunning buffet and dragged him out into the moonlight where I stood, clutching my middle, and gasping for breath.

Tossing the limp figure to the floor in a swirl of black, ragged cloak, Ergon growled, "I believe this is yours, Jandar?"

"Indeed it is," I panted. "Ergon, strike a light to yonder candelabrum, and let us see what we have caught."

The hunched little figure huddled at our feet whined and sniveled as Ergon strode to an ivory-inlaid taboret and touched a flame to the many-branched candlestick. In the milky light we perceived a scrawny, bent little man wrapped in the greasy folds of a ragged, patched cloak of black fabric.

"Cry you mercy, lords!" the little man snuffled. "If it be I have come into the wrong chamber by mistake, why—why—"

Ergon stripped the black cloak away and we peered down in amusement and curiosity at the whimpering, miserable creature that groveled before us. He was thin and scrawny and looked half-starved, with bony shanks and a huge beak of a nose, comical in a seamed and wizened face. It was impossible to guess his age, but his place in society was unmistakable.

Ergon grunted sourly, pointing to a brand burnt into the brow of the whimpering little man. "A thief," he growled. The little fellow peered up at us fearfully, his one good eye shrewd and sharp and bright as a ferret's, the other concealed by a black eye patch that lent him a rakish appearance. Lank, greasy locks fell in a tangle over a high bony brow. His thin-lipped mouth worked in stammering terror, a pointed chin adorned with a stringy tuft of ill-kempt beard. His hollow cheeks were stubbled, and the raw stench of cheap wine, raw onions, and sour garlic hovered about him, mingling with the odors of his unwashed body, and of the filthy, dilapidated rags that barely covered it.

"Not so—not so, lords, on my honor!" the one-eyed little rogue squeaked fearfully. "I am Glypto, an unemployed *chanthan,* at your honor's service!"

Ergon chuckled and cocked an amused eyebrow at this. The brand on the scrawny little rogue's brow was the Thanatorian character for *chark,* or "thief." But a *chanthan* is quite another thing, indeed. The term denotes a certain class of landless but wellborn gentlemen of the *chanar,* the warrior-caste. The term is often stretched to lend a degree of spurious dignity to the more furtive classes of Callistan society, however.

No wonder it roused a chuckle from glum, glowering Ergon. Our greasy, whimpering little captive referred to himself as a "gentleman adventurer," which was an overly polite euphemism for any sort of slinking rogue.

The scuffle had aroused Darloona. Clutching the coverlet of her couch about her, she asked what was toward. Spying her, our captive fell on his scrawny knees and lifted imploring—and none too clean—hands to her.

"Mercy—mercy for poor, starved Glypto, noble lady! Glypto meant no harm to the noble lords! Glypto mistook his way in the black of night, he—"

"Jandar, what in the world is this?" Darloona queried, her surprise giving way to amusement. I shrugged, laughing.

"An unexpected ally, my Princess! A friend who has come to extricate us from our predicament . . ."

Ergon frowned, wrinkling his bald scarlet pate. Nudging the groveling little rogue with a toe, he growled. "'Tis but a thieving rascal, Jandar! Call you this whining *horeb* 'friend'?"

"I do indeed, Ergon," I smiled. "I will hail any man as my friend, who shows me a way to get out of this gilded cage in which we are locked."

Darloona looked at me puzzledly. "But how can this little man help us?" she murmured.

"My darling," I grinned, "he got in here some-how—and unobserved, since thieves are seldom in-

vited to ply their trade in palaces. And however he
got in—surely we can get out by the same route."

Ergon's brow cleared at my words and his surly
gaze sparkled with zest at the thought of freedom.
"Of course! Devil take me for a witless fool! Here,
you—whatever your name is—we're not going to kill
you or turn you over to the guards—so cease your
everlasting whimpering before you summon them
hither with your uproar."

Glypto's snuffling was cut short, as he suddenly realized he was in no danger from us. His shrewd little
eye peered up from where he crouched, sharp yet furtive, as if hardly daring to believe his good fortune.

"Glypto the *chanthan*, my masters!" he chirped
brightly.

"Nay, 'tis Glypto the Thief, I'll wager," smiled
Darloona.

He ducked in an obsequious little bow.

"And you will have it so, gracious lady! Glypto the
Thief—the son of Glypto the Thief—the *grandson*
of Glypto the Thief—at your service, my masters!"

It was hard to keep a straight face when talking
to the little fellow; everything about him was in-
nately comical, from his ferretlike, twinkling one eye
to his enormous beak of a nose which dominated his
famished, wizened face as if in its growth, the prominent proboscis had drained his other features of
their vitality in order to sustain itself. And his
whining little voice, which either croaked like a frog
or chirped like a sparrow, itself made you chuckle.
For he spoke his Thanatorian with a drawl on the
vowels and a rasp of the consonants that sounded for
all the world like the Callistan equivalent of Cock-
ney.

"See here, Glypto," I said severely, "you are in no
danger of harm from us, so long as you do our bidding. We are held captive here, and if you assist us in
making our escape, a rich reward will be yours. . . ."

He crawled to his feet, nimbly retrieving the little hooked knife I had wrested from him, which he
restored to its accustomed place within the bundle

of sour rags that clothed his scrawny form. Even standing, the hunched, sidling little man scarcely came up to Ergon's collarbone.

"At your service, noble lords! How can Glypto the *chanthan* be of service?" he chirped inquisitively.

"We want to know how you got in here, guttersnipe," Ergon grunted. In answer, Glypto rolled his one good eye eloquently skyward. We followed his gaze. Ergon growled a curse and I groaned.

For a black opening yawned in the ceiling!

Earlier, Ergon and I had searched every inch of the apartment, thumping every foot of the walls, hoping to find a secret panel or a concealed passage of some sort, as the palaces of Thanator are often honeycombed with such. We had even rolled back the carpets and tested the floors.

But it had simply never occurred to us to try the ceiling!

The little rogue grinned and strutted, preening himself in our eyes.

"An hereditary secret, my noble lords and masters!" he crowed. "Handed down over the generations from father to son! Aye, none less than the closely guarded secret of the House of Glypto!"

"And the meal-ticket of a family of thieving rascals, I doubt me not," grunted Ergon, making as if to cuff the swaggering little fellow with a clout from the back of his hand.

Glypto cringed from the half-hearted blow, showing pointed, ratlike, yellowish teeth in a frightened snarl. But Darloona put out one hand to halt Ergon; her womanly heart was touched by the pathetic and yet amusing little man.

"Ergon, don't strike him; he will help us to escape, and we should be grateful," she said softly.

Ergon growled and spat.

"As you will, my lady. But trust the scrawny little *horeb* no further than an arm's reach away. Such as he would sell us to the guards for a copper coin!"

Glypto made an elaborate, courtly bow to my Princess, stuck out his tongue at the surly Ergon, then

pranced across the room to where the secret
trapdoor gaped in the ceiling.

"This way! This way, my masters! Permit your servant to show you the secret of the House of Glypto!"
he chortled gaily.

Darloona quickly donned her hunting garb while Ergon and I pulled on our leathern tunics, girdles, and
buskins. Two moons were aloft in the night skies of
Thanator, and the vast amber-and-ocher-banded bulk
of mighty Gordrimator (as the Callistans term their
primary, Jupiter) heaved up its mighty orb above
the horizon by the time we were ready to depart.

A knotted cord dangled down from the panel in
the ceiling, and by this we one by one ascended,
with Glypto in our rear. We found ourselves crouched
in a narrow crawl-space between the floors. It was
dark and cramped, airless and stifling, but Glypto
produced a stub of candle to which he struck a light.
By the thin, wavering illumination of this bit of
greasy wax we perceived that the narrow space between the floors consisted of heavy beams between
which thin flimsy laths, coated with plaster, formed
the ceiling. Glypto showed us how to crawl along
the beams and cautioned us against putting any
weight on the laths between these beams, warning
us that they were not strong enough to bear our
weight.

So we progressed on hands and knees, Glypto taking the forward position after carefully drawing up
the knotted line, which he untied and stowed away
beneath his rags. He also drew up and pegged shut
the trapdoor: when shut, the hairline crack in the
plaster was invisible from the room below, or so he
assured us.

The crawl-space ended in a vertical wall wherein
Glypto or his ancestors had cut a hole. Once through
this we were able to stand erect, and found ourselves
in a black and stifling passageway hollowed through
the wall of the palace. We could stand erect, but
could only go back or forward by inching along side-

ways, so narrow was the passage between the wall of
our room and that of the next apartment.

Glypto sent a chill of dread into the very marrow
of my bones when he carelessly announced that the
apartment next to ours housed none other than the
gray-robed, slant-eyed yellow dwarf who had so cleverly assisted in our capture. This personage he called
the Queen's priest and councillor, and gave us to understand that his name was Ang Chan.

I knew—although my companions did not—that
the yellow dwarf was one of the Mind Wizards of
Kuur. This I had guessed from the start, because he
was obviously of the same race as Ool the Uncanny,
who by an odd and thought-provoking coincidence
had also served Arkola the Usurper, the chief of the
Black Legion, as his priest and councillor.

And, as I had excellent cause to know, Ool had
been a natural telepath!

I had already guessed that Zamara's cunning accomplice was also a member of this mysterious race
whose emissaries appear from time to time on the
great stage of Thanatorian affairs, always in a position of enormous influence, to manipulate the flow of
events for some purpose unknown and unguessable except to themselves. Assuming the Mind Wizards to
be a race of telepaths, I suddenly understood many
things which had baffled me before. So swift had
been the succession of events, so dire the perils into
which chance had thrust us, that the struggle to
think of a solution to our predicament had occupied
my mind to the exclusion of other thoughts.

But now, quite suddenly, it came to me how Darloona and Ergon and I had been lured into outstrip-
ping our hunting party, and had been drawn into
the clump of woods where Zamara and her band had
been hidden, prepared to seize us.

We had pursued a snow-white *vanth*.

A vanth that Ergon had not been able to see!

A *vanth* that had miraculously vanished into thin
air before our very eyes, the moment we were
beneath the hidden nets!

These thoughts went tumbling through my mind
as I inched along the narrow passage between the
walls.

Suddenly my whirling brain made sense of the
chaos of mysteries into which we had been thrust.

Suddenly, one by one, the scattered pieces of the
puzzle fell into place.

Suddenly, I knew the answer to the secret!

Chapter 6

The Captor Made Captive

For I suddenly knew that the shadowy and elusive Mind Wizards could do more than just read the minds of others. They could subtly and secretly *influence* those minds, as well!

For the human mind is much more than just a center of the cognitive faculty and a storehouse of memory. It is the switchboard of the senses: therein the ears and the eyes and the other sensory organs feed the results of their surveillance to be interpreted to the brain in the great nerve centers.

The vision center, for instance, digests and arranges into pictures the information gathered by the eyesight and fed into the brain in the form of electrical impulses passed along the nerve fibers.

It suddenly occurred to me that a trained and gifted telepath might well be able to tamper with the vision center of the brain, *inducing the illusion of pictures directly to the brain—pictures the eyes themselves had not really seen at all!*

Such as the elusive white *vanth* we had followed.

The *vanth* that had led us straightway into a cunningly laid trap.

The vanth that had somehow been invisible to Ergon.

The *vanth* that had disappeared, the moment we were beneath the nets. The *vanth* that had been invisible to Ergon for the very good reason that *it had not really been there at all.*

Concealed within the copse, Ang Chan had telepathically transmitted the cleverly sustained *illusion* of a fleeing *vanth* into the unsuspecting minds of Darloona and me. Because it was we two he wished to capture.

Ergon had not been induced to see the *vanth* because Ang Chan had no reason to wish to capture him.

It was mere chance that Ergon, alone of our companions, had been at the fore of the party with my Princess and myself when we saw—or *thought* we saw—the rare white *vanth*. Not knowing why we so suddenly broke into a charge, he unthinkingly spurred his *thaptor* in order to keep up with us, and thus had been captured as well. Had not the kidnapping been timed to a split-second schedule, in order for us to be bundled off in the balloon mere instants before the remainder of the hunting party entered the copse on our heels, Ergon would doubtless have been murdered on the spot. But that would have taken a few moments—and Zamara's scheme was not timed to include those few extra moments. So it had proved best to merely take him along.

Cold perspiration burst out on my bare forearms. Ugly, faithful, loyal devoted old Ergon! He owed his very life to the fact that Zamara's scheme had not included a few seconds leeway!

Once this simple fact entered my comprehension, other pieces of the puzzle coalesced neatly. We had been housed in such curious comfort, simply because Ang Chan's quarters lay next to our own.

Obviously, our capture was the initial phase in Zamara's megalomaniac scheme of world conquest. Seizing us left Shondakor leaderless. In our absence, the Shondakorian host would weary its strength and scatter its forces hither and thither about the Great Plains, searching for the lost Prince and Princess. In this interval of disorder and confusion and dispersal of strength, the legions of Tharkol would strike in an invasion that was doubtless the second phase in Zamara's plan of conquest.

But there was more to be gained from holding Darloona and me captive—especially if you have a trained and subtle telepath on hand! We had been

housed in the apartment next to Ang Chan so that
he could read our minds while we slept or idly con-
'ersed. And in our minds lay immensely valuable in-
ormation of enormous use to any would-be conqueror,
for Darloona and I well knew the details of the defense and armaments of Shondakor, the disposition
of troops, the schedules of sentries, the flag signals—
even the passwords of the gates, which were changed
daily according to a prearranged system.

And now perspiration bedewed my brow as well. For
if Ang Chan were beyond this wall, mentally eaves-
dropping on us, he must surely by now know that we
were escaping!

I reached out and seized Glypto by the collar of
his cloak and hissed an urgent question into his ear.
He shrugged, then fumbled along the inner wall until
his sensitive fingers found some small aperture invisible to me in the uncertain light. Fitting his one
good eye on the spyhole, the little rogue peered into
the room beyond, then straightened, smirking.

"Nay, my master, the priest be not within. Oh—
aye!—now that I call it to mind, this night our holy
Empress holds a state ball to celebrate some coup or
other against the realm of Shondakor, which city,
the gossip of the taverns hath it, be the first prize
on her list of conquests," he said, offhandedly, not
dreaming that it was *our* capture which had been
the coup in question. We had seen no particular reason, as yet, to inform our involuntary little guide as
to our identities, or the reasons for our captivity.
Doubtless he assumed us to be courtiers suffering house
arrest for some displeasure we had caused the Empress. Things had happened too swiftly, perhaps, for
him to have yet noticed in the darkness and the
confusion of our scuffle, that of the three of us only
Ergon was a Perushtarian.

I relaxed a bit at the news that the suite beyond
the wall was currently unoccupied; but the hour was
very late, and surely the ball must have ended by
now and the lords and ladies of the court would be

returning to their suites. At any moment, the yellow dwarf from mysterious Kuur might enter his suite to eavesdrop on us. *At any moment, then, he could discover that we had escaped, and would raise the alarm!*

"We must be gone from this place just as soon as possible," I whispered, thinking swiftly. "Glypto, where does the passage lead to in this direction?"

He fingered his tuft of beard with nimble, greasy fingers, thoughtfully.

"Now let me think on it, my master . . . past the royal apartments of the Empress herself, aye! And thence deeper into the inner citadel—"

"And in the other direction? Swiftly, friend—every moment counts!"

"Why . . . out through the walls of the keep, of course . . . 'tis a lengthy and a winding way, I fear, but it ends at last in the sewers which honeycomb the space beneath the streets o' the city, and thus to many o' the safe and snug hidey-holes in the Thieves' Quarter. . . ."

I cursed desperately, feeling the precious moments slipping away—and with them, this last small chance of our escaping.

"No good at all . . . that way would take too long, and if Ang Chan is what I fear he is, he could find us even in the sewers . . . is there any other exit nearby?"

Glypto squinted a bright, inquisitive eye up at me, curious as to my haste. "Oh, aye, a trap in each ceiling leads down into every room, even the Empress's, though he would be a bolder *chanthan* than even Glypto who would dare to use it! *Ooff!*" he squeaked as I shook him violently, to shake his mind from these rambling reminiscences. "Aye, I'm *thinking,* lord, don't shake the breath out of my poor old bones! A nearer exit—aye! I mind me that my grandfather had a stone hollowed away at 'tother end, which lets forth on this tier. . . ."

"The *third* tier, isn't it?" I demanded suddenly, a marvelous scheme having suddenly sprung full-blown into my brain.

"Aye . . . the third tier it is."

"Where the balloon is tethered—the flying thing that carried us here?"

He nodded slowly. "Aye . . . guarded by three, or is it four, men at arms? Three, I think. . . ."

"I care not if 'twere a dozen," I said recklessly, with a grin of sheer mischief. "For the Lords of Gordrimator are with us this night! They *must* be, for at last things are going in our favor!"

Ergon's froglike face looked at me bewilderedly in the feeble light of the flickering candle stub.

"Jandar, what is toward? You're hatching some scheme, I'll wager, but 'tis past my wit to guess it straight. . . ."

"Everything will be explained in a moment," I laughed. And then another thought occurred to me —a thought so deliciously pregnant with pleasurable possibilities that I stopped short in my tracks.

"Glypto—where is the suite of this self-styled Empress of yours?" I snapped.

His wizened face was every bit as bewildered as Ergon's but there was no time to play the game of question-and-answer now. Sensing my impatience, he scuttled ahead of me down the narrow way, and showed me the position of the spyhole.

I slid the baffle aside, stopped, and fitted my eye to the tiny aperture. It took a moment for my eyes to adjust to the dimness, but then I began to make out the details of a huge room draped in silks, carpeted with rare furs, and thronged with paintings, statuettes, tapestries, and other artworks too numerous to list.

Directly in front of me, Zamara sprawled languorously on an immense low couch covered with costly furs. She wore a dazzling gown of some sparkling, expensive-looking fabric that looked like silver lamé, and a gem-studded tiara flashed about her brows, caught in her ebon tresses. As I gazed upon this scene, the Empress of Tharkol was sipping a goblet of chilled wine while a slave girl knelt before her, gently massaging her feet with some perfumed oil. Even as I watched, Zamara dismissed the servant

with a flick of her hand, turned to an immense mirror, and began lazily removing her jewels. The slave
girl scuttled out, and, my eyes searching every corner
of the room, I ascertained to my indescribable amusement and delight that Zamara was now completely
alone in her apartments.

Taking my eye from the spyhole, I seized Glypto
by the collar of his threadbare cloak.

"Where is the trapdoor in the ceiling of the
room?"

"There, lord, but—"

"Give me the candle. Ergon! Collar this rogue, and
if he squeals, teach him the weight of your hand."

"'Twill be a pleasure," Ergon growled, enveloping
the little thief in brawny arms. From behind him,
down the narrow passage, Darloona gazed at me
with amazement and wonder in her emerald eyes.

"Jandar, what is it that you plan to do?" she asked.

I blew her an airy kiss.

"Beloved, we are going to escape in style—and
we'll be carrying a little 'life insurance' along, just in
case a guard or two gets too handy with his spear!
I'll be back in just a moment, with a surprise for you
all. While I'm gone, go back down the passage and
find the exit that leads out onto this tier of the palace. If our luck is still with us, we'll find the balloon
still tethered there . . . get along, now, all of you!"

Faces mirroring their puzzlement, they crept off
down the passage while I ducked through the low rat
hole, crawled out on one of the beams, found and un-
latched the trapdoor, opened it and swung through,
to drop as soundlessly as a great cat to the floor directly behind the would-be Empress of Callisto!

Chapter 7

The Plaything of the Winds

Ergon's mind swirled in baffled confusion, unable to
discern from my gleeful and reckless grin and light-
hearted words whatever plan or scheme it was I was
hatching. But the loyal fellow did not pause to question my odd directions for a moment. Ugly, strong,
and as utterly faithful as a huge mastiff, the burly-
shouldered Perushtarian who had been my fellow
slave in the pens of Narouk, my comrade among the
gladiators of Zanadar, and who would remain my
dogged and stouthearted friend to the last throb of
his indomitable heart, turned and crept off down
the winding passage, half-dragging our little guttersnipe of a guide in the grip of his powerful hands.

In a few moments Glypto, eyes goggling with terror, half strangled in the unthinking grip of those
massive hands, timidly flapped his hands until he had
attracted the attention of the surly, bandy-legged
bald giant who bore him along as effortlessly as if he
were a flimsy doll.

"What is it?" Ergon growled.

"The p-panel, noble lord! The p-panel that leads
out to the p-parapet!" Glypto whined.

"Open it, then, rogue!"

"M-might it n-not be b-better to peer out first,
and view the l-lay of the l-land?" the thief whimpered. Gruffly, Ergon nodded; loosening the bruising
grip of his great paws, he permitted the scrawny
thief to dig loose a morsel of clay, exposing a chink
in the outer wall. Peering out, Ergon stifled a gasp of
delight. Suddenly he contemplated the beauty of my
scheme . . . for there before him, tethered to the

low parapet, swung the capacious basket which had
borne us thither on the winds, and above it, the
huge gasbag of the balloon swelled against the glim-
mer of the many moons.

He understood that it was my intent to escape
from Tharkol by means of the very instrument that
had brought us here—the balloon!

True, three guards were stationed there to protect
the flying vehicle of their Empress against any mischief which might befall. But, wrapped in warm
cloaks, they huddled in the shelter of the parapet
against the cold blast of the night wind, stealing
forty winks against the next approach of their captain, walking his nightly rounds. Unsuspectingly,
they dozed if but lightly; and Ergon's hands itched
to pounce upon them and batter them senseless, as
he would have done regardless, even had they been
twice their number.

He glanced speculatively about the broad terrace,
which was clearly lit by the several moons and the
mighty bulk of Jupiter itself. While I was about my
mysterious business at the other terminus of the
secret passageway, Ergon perceived no reason why he
should not ready things at this end, so that all
would be prepared for our departure as soon as I rejoined their company.

"Open it, cur," he growled.

The terrified little thief did not dare disobey: he
winced in the crushing grip of this grim colossus and
did not care to dispute with him, having already felt
the iron weight of those calloused paws. With trembling fingers, sniveling a little in the extremity of
his fear, Glypto disengaged the several flat pegs that
held the hollow shell of stone in place beside its
more solid fellows. The hidden door fell open.

Ergon thrust the shrinking thief into the ready
grasp of Darloona, curtly bidding her watch he utter
no single squeal or slip away. Then in three great
bounds, the burly Perushtarian was upon the dozing
guards.

The poor fellows never knew what hit them; in

the weeks that followed, while nursing their hurts in the barracks infirmary, the three no doubt oft discussed whether it had been some night-wandering demon had swooped upon them from the windy skies, or mayhap some winged and dreadful predator of the heavens—a *Ghastozar* perchance—had torn them from their rest, hurling them to the terrace far below. They probably decided on the *Ghastozar;* but it was really only a surly-tempered Perushtarian who felt like a bit of exercise.

Having tossed the stupefied guards one by one over the parapet, after first ripping from their harnesses the swords and daggers they wore, Ergon dusted his hands with a grunt of satisfaction, and beckoned to Darloona to join him.

Accompanied by Glypto, the Princess swiftly crossed the terrace and climbed into the basket while Ergon held it steady. Then he handed in to her the several weapons he had so rudely harvested, and, naked sword clenched in one burly fist, held himself ready to sever the ropes which anchored the balloon to the balustrade and launch us forth on the winds the moment I had come.

He hesitated only a moment over the cowering Glypto. Then, as I had said nothing about turning the little rogue loose, he scooped up the squealing little man and tossed him into the basket beside my Princess.

Scarce was this done but I appeared in the entrance, a writhing bundle, wrapped in a silken coverlet, squirming in my arms. I climbed quickly into the basket, tossed my feebly-wriggling burden into one corner, beckoned at Ergon to join us, and curtly bade him cut the anchor cable. Moonlight flashed on the steely mirror of his blade as he swung it hissing down, chopping through the cable.

The basket gave a sickening lurch, and we were away!

The fourth tier swept down upon us, but we cleared it. Then the ziggurat-like citadel swam away beneath us, and the city itself, in a blur of streets,

squares, and rooftops. Towers whistled by us as we
soared above the world, mounting higher and higher
in the grip of powerful winds.

And in another breath the walls of Tharkol reced-
ed from us in the moonlit dark, and we were free at
last!

Laughing in mingled delight and relief, Darloona
flung her arms about my neck. I crushed her to me
and kissed her so thoroughly that she gasped.

She asked me something then, but the rushing
winds snatched her words away as soon as they were
uttered. Shouting louder, she asked me what I had
gone back to do.

"Remember I said I thought it would be nice to
carry along a little 'life insurance' with us on our
journey?" I yelled back. The single universal language
spoken across the breadth of Thanator by the several
races which share the Jungle Moon between them,
unfortunately lacks a term for the concept, so I was
forced to paraphrase it so broadly that its meaning
eluded her comprehension. She shrugged, not under-
standing. I opened my mouth to attempt a further
explanation, then grinned and gave it up.

Far easier, thought I, to illustrate the notion by
action. Gesturing to catch her eye, I stooped and
pulled back the flap of the silk-enveloped bundle I
had so unceremoniously tossed into a corner of the
swaying basket.

Now uncovered, a face looked up at us, flushed and
furious, ripe lips biting frenziedly against my hasty
gag.

Darloona's eyes widened with shock and amazement, then glowed with mischievous humor. She
plucked at Ergon's sleeve, calling to his attention
the captive which writhed and wriggled on the floor
of the basket, glaring up at us with incandescent
rage and hatred.

He looked, and laughed. Beyond him, little
Glypto, cowering in panic in the far corner peeped
at our captive through his fingers, then howled dis-
mally, and covered his face in a very ecstasy of dread.

For, bound and gagged on the floor of the basket, Zamara of Tharkol glared up at us with murder in her blazing eyes!

Dawn was too near for any of us to think of trying to catch a bit of sleep—even if such had been possible, given the violence wherewith the raging winds tossed our basket about in sickening swoops.

It would have been completely impossible to have striven to maneuver or pilot the balloon, such was the force of the gale, so we did not even bother trying to do so. Let the winds carry us where they might; every moment took us further and further from the city of our enemies. And, rage how they would, the winds would die at last, and we could then take the balloon under control and guide it home to Shondakor.

Or so we thought, anyway.

Looking back on that dizzy voyage through the skies, I think we were all a little drunk with triumph. Our miraculous good luck in escaping from the Tharkolians raised our spirits giddily. We had been sunken in gloom and depression; now, having succeeded in escaping from the very stronghold of our enemies, we were all a little intoxicated, and thought ourselves the darlings of the gods.

The most deliciously hilarious thing about our escape was, of course, the manner in which we had turned the tables on our prideful and super-confident captors. Chief among whom was the self-styled "Empress of Callisto." The captor had herself become the captive, and we had reversed our roles with a vengeance! We would not have been human if the situation had not delighted us so.

As for Zamara, the poor girl was wild and frothing with fury. She fought and fought, wriggling like a wildcat, in a futile struggle against the silken scarves wherewith I had hastily but stoutly bound her wrists and ankles when I dropped from the ceiling to seize her at her vanity table.

It had been Zamara's pleasure to seize and bind us

and carry us off unceremoniously. But now the tables had turned, and it was the divine Empress who had been snatched up, securely trussed, and tossed into the basket, to be whisked away to an unguessable fate.

A lifetime of unbridled pride and vaunting ambition had made the red-skinned young woman a thoroughly spoiled brat. This was probably the first time since childhood that any hand had been raised in violence against her pampered and princely person. She fought, kicked, and squirmed against her bonds until her furious strength was exhausted. Then she gave way to her misery, and loosed a storm burst of tears. Relenting, Darloona bade us remove her gag, but when Ergon stooped to do so she sunk her sharp white teeth in the flesh of his hand and bespattered us with a torrent of curses that would have won her the awed admiration of a longshoreman.

We let her rant and rage and weep as she would, ignoring it, for in truth the wind whipped away the worst part of her sulphurous language. Little Glypto, doubtless a connoisseur of oaths, sat fascinated, drinking it all in. Doubtless he committed to memory some of the more anatomically ingenious of her suggestions as to our ancestry and personal habits, wherewith to regale his criminous compatriots when next he mingled among the lower classes of the Thieves' Quarter.

But we were humane in our treatment of Zamara, and I loosened her bonds and made her as comfortable as I could, without of course freeing her hands.

"You stinking *horeb*'s-dung! You spittle of diseased maggots! You reeking gob of slime cast by a filthy reptile! You vile and loathsome offspring of a self-impregnating *xanga!* You toad's-dropping—you offal of garbage-devouring *zulths!* You—you—you dare touch with your fetid paws the sacred person of the divine Empress to whom the Lords of Gordrimator have given the very world!"

She raved on, tears pouring down smudged and dirty cheeks. I, of course, paid no attention to her tempestuous tongue. The poor girl was more than half mad, of course, to take unto herself divine prerogatives. Listening, Darloona half smiled.

"Perhaps we should replace the gag after all," she grinned.

Dawn broke, a blaze of gold. I went to the rim of the basket and stared about. Beneath us rushed an unknown country, wooded hills and vast rolling meadows. It looked nothing at all like the level plains that stretched between Tharkol and Shondakor: had the winds perchance carried us in the opposite direction—further into the east? The maps of the known surface of Thanator ended a few leagues to the east of Tharkol; beyond the borders of the known hemisphere stretched the unexplored and unmapped vastnesses of the far side of Callisto, which remained a region of shadowy and legended mystery.

For hours the balloon had flown through the darkness, a helpless plaything of the winds. How far had the winds carried us in that time, and in which direction?

And the winds still howled at gale force! If we were indeed traveling east, we would be borne into the unknown further side of the Jungle Moon before we could manage to descend!

Just then Ergon called my name.

I looked to where he stood across the basket from me, craning his head back, staring up into the sky, a strained expression on his froglike visage.

"What's the matter now?" I asked. "Haven't we got enough trouble?"

"It would seem that more lies in store for us," he said grimly. "Look!"

I looked up . . . to see a hideous, bat-winged shape hurtling down upon us from the brilliant regions of the upper sky.

It was a gigantic *Ghastozar*—the most dreaded predator of the skies of Thanator.

And it was coming straight for us—

Chapter 8

The Terror of the Skies

"*Aiiiiii!*" Glypto shrieked, cowering on the floor of the basket, curling into a ball as if to make of himself the smallest possible target.

As for myself, my heart sank into my boots, and stayed there. I did not in the least blame the scrawny little rascal for squealing like a stuck pig as the flying monster swept down upon us.

For the *ghastozar* is one of the most horrible of the many grisly monstrosities that prowl the Jungle Moon. A flying reptile with vast membranous wings and terrible claws, it resembles nothing so closely as the terrific flying dragon of Earth's remote dawn age—the dread pterodactyl.

It measures fully twenty feet from fanged snout to barbed and viciously-whipping tail, and the steely power of its gliding thews is such that it has been known to rip a fully grown *deltagar* to shreds. Since a *deltagar* is a monster resembling two or three saber-toothed tigers rolled into one ferocious avalanche of murderous fury, you can easily form an estimate of how formidable was the flying doom that now swept down upon us.

There was literally nothing we could do to protect ourselves. We were armed only with the swords and daggers Ergon had stripped from the guards before he tossed them over the parapet, and against the fury of the mighty *ghastozar*, these were as so many toothpicks. If the Tharkolians had been armed with bows and arrows or with the light throwing spear used by Ku Thad huntsmen, it would have been quite a different story. Then we should have

had at least a fighting chance against the winged
dragon-monster of the skies. And a fighting chance is
all I have ever asked of the inscrutable fate that rules
our destiny.

But they had not been so armed, and our chances
of fighting off the *ghastozar* were slim, and our hopes
for survival few.

Ergon knew this as well as I: we exchanged a grim
look, but did not discuss the situation aloud in order
to spare the women unnecessary fear. And now I regretted having carried off Zamara, thus exposing her
to this horrible danger. The poor, deluded Tharkolian princess was mad, and had made herself our implacable enemy, but, having been lucky enough to escape from her clutches, and having by now left the
city of Tharkol far behind, it was cruel of us to have
thrust her into such peril. She could no longer do us
ill, and I have never had the heart for vengeance.

Perhaps most of all, in a way, I regretted that little Glypto had been carried off with us and now
faced a hideous doom in the jaws of the monster
ghastozar. The little rogue had done us no ill at all,
had in fact been the very instrument of our escape,
and it was a sorry recompense for his services. But
there was nothing I could do about it now, and
soon—very soon—my regrets would end as would my
life.

As these thoughts spun through my brain the flying
monster hurtled past us, curved about and flew
towards us again. I do not know why the brute had
not struck us on his first passage: he was hunting,
which meant he was hungry. And we were prey.

Again he flashed past us without striking, and this
time he halted and flapped around us in a slow circle,
turning his hideous beaked head first to the one side
then to the other, peering at us with little red eyes
in which ravenous blood lust vied oddly with a hesi-
tancy I did not understand.

"Why does he not strike and have done with it?"
Ergon growled at my side. I shrugged helplessly.

And then, quite suddenly, the answer came to me.

The monster was puzzled! He had never seen any-thing like the floating balloon and its dangling bas-ket before. He was not certain what we were, nor whether we were good to eat. He was—*curious!*

He flapped about, circling us at a safe distance, eyeing us warily. The dim, small brain of the flying reptile was baffled by our ungainly shape and our pecu-liar odor. He was hesitant to attack us, not knowing what we were, how we might defend ourselves, nor even if we were edible.

And suddenly, I knew we had a chance.

Galvanized into action, I let out a yip, attracting the attention of the others.

"Yell—wave your arms—make noise!" I com-manded. And, suiting my actions to my words, I be-gan capering about the basket, screeching at the top of my lungs and windmilling my arms in a wild, maniacal fashion.

The *ghastozar* flinched aside and withdrew, peer-ing at me warily.

Ergon and Darloona instantly got the idea and sensed my thoughts. Solemn, glum-faced Ergon began an awkward dance from side to side, booming out loud cries and my Princess yelled with all the lung-power at her command. I could have laughed at Er-gon's self-conscious expression, as he soberly pranced about, waving his arms like a maniac, had not the situation been so serious and our danger so deadly.

The balloon wobbled and swung widely from side to side, almost pitching us out. The uproar we three made was deafening. And, true to my theory, the flying reptile withdrew to a safer distance, but con-tinued to eye us in a puzzled fashion.

Never in all its days had the winged predator of the skies seen a flying thing that bobbed about so madly and voiced such a cacaphonous battle cry. It was baffled. And it began to get angry. My plan, it seemed, was not without its flaws. The tiny brain of the *ghastozar* had room for only one thought or emotion at a time. Wary puzzlement had driven out hunger; and now anger drove out wariness.

It swung towards us, fanged jaws agape, striking out with bared bird claws. At the last possible moment it swept to one side, but one flashing claw caught the swinging basket a mighty buffet, knocking us from our feet.

I staggered backwards, the rim of the basket striking me in the backs of the knees, and fell over the side!

A dizzy vista of grassy plains and wooded hills flashed before my eyes as I fell like a stone.

My hands thrust out automatically, clutching on empty air.

Then something slapped me across the face. I snatched at it with that utter desperation wherewith a drowning man is said to clutch at a straw.

In my case, however, the "straw" proved to be the end of a dangling line. It was the rope whereby the Tharkolians had tied down the balloon, anchoring it to the palace tier, but only later in retrospect did I manage to identify it. When Ergon had hacked it through, cutting the balloon loose, the severed line hung free. It was the end of this that my desperate hands now encountered and to which I clung by one hand with all my strength.

I hung about eleven or twelve feet below the basket, clinging to the very end of the line with both hands by now. The world swung giddily beneath my heels; the wind tore at me with impalpable fingers, screaming in my ears like a banshee as I clung for dear life to the end of the line.

Peering up I saw a row of frightened faces staring down at me from the edge of the basket. Ergon had his wide, froggish mouth open and was yelling something inaudible to me. Darloona was pale and wide-eyed, staring down at me, her knuckles pressed against parted lips. Even little Glypto was there, his scrawny, beak-nosed face white with terror.

As for myself, I must confess to feeling no fear at all. This is not vapid braggadocio, nor am I attempting to portray myself in an heroic light. Indeed, if anything, I felt furious and embarrassed at having fallen out of the basket like a stumble-footed clown. No, I have never thought of myself as being particularly heroic. It has always been my sorry lot to get into trouble, from which I then have to extricate myself as best I can. It has always seemed to me that I have simply done whatever seemed the only thing to do at the time, and generally in such hazardous or precarious positions as my present plight, I have simply been too busy trying to figure out what to do to have sufficient leisure in which to be afraid.

Looking backward on such moments, having somehow or other escaped from them, I have usually been ludicrously weak-kneed with reaction. After the danger is past, then you have plenty of time to be frightened at the danger. But while you are suffering through it you just haven't got time enough for fear.

I have often wondered if other men who have led exciting lives of action and peril have found this to be true, or if the experience is uniquely my own.

At any rate, I was boilingly angry at my ludicrous position. I began trying to climb up the rope, but this proved very difficult to do. Each time I shifted my weight, the free-hanging basket swung widely to one side while I, hanging like a weight at the end of the dangling line, swung in the opposite direction. The dizzying business of swinging about, the vertiginous vista of hilltops spinning madly below my heels, the screaming wind that buffeted and tore at me, combined to make it difficult and dangerous to try to climb the rope hand over hand.

But there was nothing else to do.

And then another factor entered into the situation to further complicate it. And that was the *ghastozar* itself.

The flying reptile had noted my fall from the basket, and now as I swung temptingly to and fro like a fat worm on a fishhook, the winged monster made a savage stab at me.

Fanged jaws snapped sickeningly close to my legs as the thing whirled by. It passed so near me that the wind of its passage flung me about in a dizzy whirl. I kicked out with both bootheels the next time it came at me and I think it must have gotten a kick in the head for it flinched aside, shaking its head numbly.

As it veered away one great black batlike wing dealt me a terrific blow.

Stunned for a moment, my grip on the line was loosened.

And I fell free.

For a dreadful, endless moment the sky was beneath me and the world was far above.

Then my legs slammed into something and I instinctively clung to it with all the strength of my desperation.

My eyes were weeping from the stinging wind, and I could see nothing. I had come crashing down atop something and the impact drove the wind out of my lungs. Gasping for breath, blinking blearily, I clung blindly to whatever it was that I had fallen astride.

A moment later my vision cleared and I sucked air into my panting lungs and saw what it was that I had landed upon.

And then it was that I felt fear, you may be certain.

Numbing fear . . . hopeless fear . . . such as I have seldom known, and would prefer never to experience again.

For I found myself seated astride a rounded, enormous bulk, my legs clasped about its under-curve, and my arms wrapped tightly and desperately about a long extension that branched off the parent body. It was rough and cold to the touch, with a leathery texture most peculiar and difficult to identify.

In another breath, however, the world righted itself and I had time to discover my predicament. And, believe me, dear reader, the blood ran cold in my veins.

For I had fallen upon the ghastozar, *and was now seated astride the dreadful monster of the skies!*

Book Three

BORAK THE YATHOON

Chapter 9

The Scarlet Arrow

Wrapping my arms about the snaky neck of the *ghas-tozar*, I clung to the back of the monster with desperate strength.

Below my heels the wooded landscape swept by at dizzying speed. Above me, the balloon careened along, basket swaying drunkenly from side to side, a helpless plaything of the rushing winds.

A terrible fear possessed me. I could taste it, sour and metallic, in the back of my mouth. Fear, I discovered, had an oily taste like brass.

My heart thudded painfully against my ribs. I panted for breath, lungs burning. The wind lashed my bare arms and thighs, whipping my hair, making my eyes water until my vision blurred.

Would this terrible voyage into the unknown never end?

And how else *could* it end . . . save in death?

The flying monster flapped its ungainly bulk in wide circles around the balloon. Gradually it penetrated into the dim, small brain of the winged reptile that it bore an unaccustomed weight on its back. The dreadful head craned about, peering at me, fanged jaws agape. Eyes of red flame glared into mine—eyes empty of thought, eyes filled with blood lust and furious rage.

I crouched lower, clinging between the brute's shoulders, burying my face in the base of its neck. It craned and twisted, madly striving to reach me with those yawning jaws that bristled with razor-sharp fangs. Gusts of putrid breath blew in my face sickeningly. The clash of those chomping teeth rang in my ears. Droplets of drooling spittle sprayed my arms and shoulders as the maddened *ghastozar* strove in vain to reach me. But its coiling, snaky neck could not quite twist back far enough so that those hungry jaws could sink in my flesh, to rip and tear.

In its wild, careening flight, the *ghastozar* had forgotten about the runaway balloon and as it strove to get at me its outstretched wings struck and snagged the gasbag.

The wings of the flying monster, like those of the terrene bat it so resembles, or those of the prehistoric pterodactyl it resembles even more closely, evolved from the forepaws of the brute. The ribs of the wing are really elongated fingers, ending in hooked and razory claws, with thin membrane stretched between them, taut as a drumhead.

It was one of these fishhook claws that brushed the wobbling gasbag—

Brushed—*and snagged and tore!*

So close were we at that instant that I heard Ergon's deep voice, cursing, and Darloona's shrill cry of alarm.

In the very next moment, the maddened monster veered away in a long gull-like curve to one side. But the damage was done. A long rip, about two feet in length, scored the smooth, tight rondure of the gasbag. And the vapor gushed from it in a torrent.

I have no idea what the gas was that Zamara employed in her aerial invention, whether it was hydrogen or helium or some gas peculiar to Callisto and unknown on my native planet. But it was lighter than air and served to lift the balloon aloft. Now, as the unknown gas rushed from the bag, it shrank in upon itself, wrinkling, sagging, losing tension. It began to empty swiftly, and as it did so the balloon began to sink toward the ground below.

I had a horrible picture in my mind—a vision of the balloon hurtling into rugged, wooded hills at terrific velocity, mangling and crippling its helpless occupants. And, surely, had the vessel continued at its original speed, the flight would have ended with tragic swiftness.

But as the vapor escaped from the collapsing gasbag, the balloon sank toward the ground. As it lost altitude, it left the region of the howling winds, and fell into a layer of calmer air. Thus its velocity lessened rapidly as it sank lower and lower.

And by this time we had left the wooded hills behind and were flying over an immense region of level, grassy plains—doubtless an eastern extension of the Great Plains of Haratha. We could see clearly by this time for dawn had long since lit the vaporous skies to luminous golden fires. We had flown all night in the grip of the winds, it seemed.

So when the balloon eventually struck the ground, it would come down in the flat plains. And there was a good chance that those within the basket would survive unharmed.

My aerial steed, stung to fury by the unexpected and maddening sensation of being ridden by one of the little two-legged creatures from the flying basket, lost interest in the rapidly deflating balloon. It soared about the skies, hurling through a series of aerial maneuvers designed to dislodge me from my precarious seat between its shoulders. I have never ridden a "bucking bronco" in a rodeo, but I have no doubt the experience was similar. I clung to the enraged reptile, retaining my seat at times with the greatest difficulty.

And suddenly I found myself flying over an immense cortege that wound across the plains for miles, or so it seemed. Beaked, restive *thaptors* drew great rolling chariots or huge wains laden with folded tents, stores, and gear. In the forefront of the vast procession, and to either side, an armed host of peculiar beings rode astride the bird-horses. These warriors were naked, their attenuated limbs clad in a shiny chitin like the shell of the lobster. Knobbed antennae sprouted from the horny ovoid casques that were their heads, and eyes like globular clusters of black crystals peered solemnly skyward to observe my flight.

I recognized the procession for one of the vast migrations of the Yathoon Horde, a barbaric race of coldly intelligent but humorless and emotionless giant creatures evolved to reason from some species of insect as we humans are from the higher primates.

During the first weeks after my arrival on Callisto I had been taken captive by one such clan of the Yathoon, and during that captivity I was instructed in the one language spoken universally across the face of the Jungle Moon by all intelligent races. My memories of that period of enslavement, which was brief in term, are clear and sharp, because it was during that interval in my adventures on this mysterious world that I made my first friend and first met the woman to whom my heart was sworn.

But I had not the slightest desire to repeat the experience again, for the second time I should probably not be so lucky as the first. That is, I had established friendship with a Yathoon chieftain, Koja, whom I had rescued from certain death. The cold, logical, emotionless arthropod had learned from me a concept alien to his weird, uncanny kind: the concept of friendship. Thus, to repay me for my kindness in saving his life, he had set me free. Had things not eventuated in that manner, I might to this day be a naked, hopeless slave of the nomad insectoid warriors.

We swept across the Yathoon line of march, and the mighty procession halted in its tracks to observe this curious phenomenon. Never had the Yathoon warriors seen a human riding a monster *ghastozar* through the skies as if it were a *thaptor*. And doubtless, in their cool, unemotional way, the arthropods were curious.

I had by now lost sight of the balloon. Perhaps it had come down somewhere behind me; at least it was no longer visible aloft. I was grateful for this small favor from the inscrutable fates, for the sight of the drifting balloon with its basketful of human riders would have puzzled and intrigued the Yathoon yet further.

As it was, a party of mounted warriors detached itself from the main body of the nomads and rode across the plains in pursuit of the aerial dragon and its human rider.

The bird-horses of Callisto are capable of bursts of surprising speed, as I have mentioned elsewhere, but are seldom able to sustain it for long. And the winged dragon upon whose back I rode could easily outdistance them, I knew. Thus I expected the nomad warrior troop to fall back after a time.

This, however, did not happen. My reptilian steed was flying sluggishly, and was descending lower and lower. Vast, ragged batlike wings drummed and boomed, flapping like sails. Perhaps the brute was wearying rapidly from my unexpected weight—there are few flying creatures on this world who could bear two hundred pounds of human rider without tiring. Or perhaps . . .

But then I saw the cause.

I had not seen it happen, but one of the Yathoon chieftains had loosed a shaft against my winged and monstrous steed.

The war bows of the Yathoon Horde are terrible engines of murderous might. They are far bigger and stronger than terrene bows, and can drive the deadly three-foot-long arrows for hundreds of yards with unerring accuracy. Something in the peculiar muscular construction of the solemn arthropods makes them master archers: in this particular warrior art they far surpass their human brothers.

A scarlet arrow transfixed the skull of the ghastozar.

Eyes glazed, bloody froth bubbling from gaping jaws, the monster sagged towards the ground with a dizzying lurch.

Even so terrible an injury might not have slain the *ghastozar* at once, had it not been for the dread venom wherewith the Yathoon warriors anoint their arrows.

It is a nerve poison which attacks the major ganglia of the brain and nervous system with frightful speed. A human, or another Yathoon, struck or even nicked by these poisoned shafts will collapse in a fraction of a second. But the monster reptile, with its sluggish little brain, had managed to sustain its flight and to remain aloft for perhaps ten minutes.

But it could do so no longer.

Folding its vast wings, the dying reptile fell like a plummet. I sprang clear just before it struck the surface of the plains with a sickening impact and the crunch and snap of breaking bones.

I owe my continued existence in this life to two chance factors. One was that we were flying only thirty or forty feet above the ground when the *ghastozar* fell. The other was that the plain was carpeted in a thick, springy growth of long, thick grasses which broke my fall and cushioned me against the impact. As it was, however, I was stunned and groggy and lay sprawled on the ground for a moment before I was able to stagger to my feet.

The world swam about me in dizzy circles. I was lame in every muscle; covered with bruises; and half shaken out of my wits.

However—I yet lived!

I had not thought to elude death for long, mounted on the back of the maddened and ravenous pterodactyl. Chance or luck or inscrutable fate had once again preserved me from certain death. I forced a grin. I didn't mind being the darling of the gods, but I wished they didn't play so roughly with their toys!

The thud of clawed feet drumming against the turf roused me from my stupor. I looked up to see the Yathoon party advancing rapidly towards me. The foremost warrior, an immense creature who must have stood nine feet tall, still had his bow strung and a second scarlet arrow, its bladed barb smeared with nerve poison, nocked and ready to let fly at my breast.

I held my hands well away from my weapons, as the nomad warriors came up to me, circled about me, and halted. They formed a great open ring, with myself at the center.

They were armed with huge spears, tufted with feathers, twelve feet from bronze-shod butt to wickedly barbed point; with deadly eight-foot-long whip swords, whereof the Yathoon are undisputed masters; and with bows and arrows.

And I had only the rapier which Ergon had taken from the guards.

Thirteen fully armed Yathoon savages to one lone human warrior: it was not the fairest of odds. I did not even have a fighting chance. I pride myself on being a master swordsman, and I have been told that I am one of the finest men with the blade on this planet.

But I didn't really have a chance of defending myself. And on such occasions I have found it wisest to yield to overwhelming numbers in a grimly philosophical way, hoping for a chance to escape later on.

This is not really a question of bravery, but one of commonsense. On the one hand lay certain death, on the other an unknown future. Who could say what opportunities for escape or rescue that future might hold?

So I surrendered and let them strip me of my weapon.

But I didn't like doing it. Surrender, even against insurmountable odds, always rankles.

I was now at the whim of the Yathoon chieftain. Or such I assumed him to be, from the richness of his weapons and accouterments and the servile, obsequious manner in which the others treated him.

He sat in the saddle, scarlet arrow nocked and pointed at my breast, and red murder was in his inscrutable jeweled eyes.

His chitinous visage was unreadable, his black crystalline eyes held no emotion. Then, after a moment, he lowered the bow and relaxed the tension in the bowstring.

"What manner of creature are you?" asked Borak the Yathoon.

I Become a Possession

There was nothing else to do, so I decided to put a bold front on the situation. I faced him squarely, arms folded upon my breast, now that his underlings had disarmed me.

"I am a warrior, and a chieftain like yourself," I said calmly.

He eyed me solemnly.

"That well may be," he said in his harsh metallic voice. "But never in all my days have I set eyes upon a being such as yourself, with such odd colorations of eyes and hair and hue of skin."

He was quite right, of course. With my straw-blond hair, the clear blue eyes of my Danish mother, and my fair skin which had borne a rich tan from the daylight of Callisto, I am unique among all the peoples of this world. I continued to put a bold front on it, however, and dissembled without seeming to do so.

"I am a stranger from a far-off land," I said, "and, so far as I know, I am the first member of my race to penetrate into these regions."

He absorbed this in a ruminative silence. Of course, I had told him nothing more than the strict truth. As the country of my birth was, at that moment, something like 387,930,000 miles away, it could indeed be most aptly described as "far-off."

"What is your name and your present allegiance?" he demanded tonelessly.

"My name is . . . Darjan, and I am in the service of Shondakor the Golden," I replied. I doubt if the Yathoon even noticed my slight hesitation before giving a version of my name which I had previously employed when captured by Perushtarian slavers from Narouk. My reasons for employing a pseudonym are simple. By now the name of Jandar is known the breadth of Thanator as the hero of a thousand daring exploits of valor and conquest. It seemed prudent to adopt a name unknown to any, for I never knew when I might encounter an old enemy who still nursed an ancient grudge.

He absorbed this in thoughtful silence; then—"You are strayed far indeed from the realm you serve," he muttered. I nodded.

"I am on a mission of great importance for the Princess of my city, and have been unfortunate enough to become lost," I said.

"How come you ride the *ghastozar?*" he inquired. "If the warrior legions of the Ku Thad have domesticated the dragon of the skies, I have yet to learn of it."

I shrugged helplessly.

"Lost and wandering, my party was attacked by a hunting *ghastozar* and I was carried off by the monster. I managed to loosen myself from its claws and climb astride its shoulders and was about to attempt to wound the brute with my sword and bring it down when you accomplished the task for me with your arrow."

He said nothing. I stood, forcing a pretense of calm self-assurance, although the sweat was trickling down my sides beneath my leather tunic.

Clearing my throat a bit, I said into the silence: "I am very grateful that you have rescued me from the beast, and offer you the gratitude of Royal Shondakor. If you will permit it, I will now be upon my way, for the message I bear on behalf of the Throne of Shondakor is one of inestimable importance."

"You mean to traverse the Great Plains afoot and alone?" he asked.

"There is no other way," I said. "I have no currency wherewith to purchase a mount, and could hardly impose on your kindness and generosity by asking for the loan of a steed."

He made no reply, but sat staring at me expressionlessly. All about me his warriors stood or sat their saddles, bending upon me their inscrutable gaze in a tense silence.

A silence that began to seem ominous . . .

"May I ask the name of him to whom I am indebted?" I ventured.

"I am Borak, a *komor* of the Horde," he said. A *komor* is a rank akin to chieftain in the military aristocracy of the Yathoon nation; a chieftain leads a retinue of warriors and is responsible for a section of the Horde in war. There are sometimes as many as sixteen or twenty *komors* in any given Yathoon clan, depending on its size and might, and these serve directly under the *akka-komor*, or high-chieftain, who is inferior only to the *Arkon* or "warlord."

"Then I am indebted to Borak the *komor*," I said. I used the word *uhorz* which connotes indebtedness; it happens to be one of the few feelings akin to friendship or gratefulness that are known to the cold, unemotional Yathoon.

"And now . . . if I may . . . I must be about my journey. I have a long way to travel, and my mission is one of the utmost importance," I said. It was worth a try, anyway.

But not this time.

"Your mission, whatever it may have been, ends here," he said harshly. "I care naught for Shondakor the Golden, whose power does not extend to the Great Plains. You are now an *amatar* of Borak the chieftain; bind him!"

They bore me back to the main body of the Horde, a helpless prisoner, my wrists bound behind my back with thongs. I was sunk in a black mood of depression, and yet my position, grim as it was, was not without a certain touch of humor. For I knew why Borak had made me captive—it was because of my yellow hair, blue eyes, and fair, tanned skin. I was a creature unique in his experience—a rare object, a curiosity. And that made me a thing of value in Borak's way of thinking!

The Yathoon are very low on the scale of civilization; they are barbarians, nomads, like the Mongols or Tartars of Earth's ancient history. They wander the plains in migrant clans, scorning to dwell in cities, and hence their culture is extremely primitive because they have never had the leisure to develop or discover the civilized arts. They neither read nor write, and thus have no literature, not even songs or sagas. Since they do not indulge in trade, they have no use for money and no conception of a system of currency. But, for all the world like great solemn jackdaws or pack rats, they prize their individual hoard of treasures.

These treasures are sometimes gems and precious metals, but not always. They can be comprised of anything rare or unusual or curious: a bright feather, an oddly colored pebble, a bone, a bit of shell. I, with my peculiar coloration, was just another curio to their primitive way of thinking. Thus I was not even so high in the social scale as to have the dignity of being a captive or a slave. I was an *amatar*—a "possession"—a soulless thing!

And where the element of humor entered into my condition, was that this was the second time that this had happened to me—and for precisely the same reason. For during my first period of captivity in the Yathoon Horde I had been captured for the same reason—my peculiar coloring!

Once the war party rejoined the main body of the Horde, the vast number of warriors and animals rumbled slowly into the march again, bearing me with them, lightly but securely trussed and tossed into one of the huge wains that belonged to Borak's retinue. The Horde was coming out of the extreme south, wandering north and east, and from this I gathered that they were returning from one of their periodic visits to the Black Mountains near the southern pole of Callisto.

Somewhere in those unknown mountains, in a
Secret Valley whose whereabouts is jealously hidden,
reside the females and the young of the Yathoon nation. The warrior clans roam the Great Plains, hunting meat and warring on each other, but periodi-
cally they journey south to the Secret Valley, the
hidden heartland of their race, where, under a never-
broken truce, the warriors of fiercely rival clans min-
gle peacefully for a time. There they breed and there
the females rear their young.

A strange, savage, grim people, the Yathoon! They
know not the meaning of peace or friendship or love
or fatherhood. Eternally at war with each other and
with all other people of this Jungle Moon, they live
out their stark, humorless lives like cold machines,
devoid of kindness or loyalty or worship or comradeship or any of the softer, warmer, more human emo-
tions and values that make life worth living for such
as we. Almost I could find it within my heart to
pity them. . . .

However, the grim emotionlessness of the
Yathoon has another side beyond mere deprivation.
If they know not love or kindness or mercy, at least
they are equally immune to jealousy or hatred or cru-
elty. Unlike those same Mongols and Tartars to
whom I have just compared them, the Yathoon
never torture their victims and take no pleasure in
the sufferings of others.

So my captivity would be lighter and less perilous
than it might have been, had I been taken prisoner
by one of the more "civilized" of the human races of
Thanator, among whom torture is common. I re-
called the high civilization of the Zanadarians to
whom, as to the ancient Romans of my own world,
savage and bloody gladiatorial games were a popular
form of entertainment; or the sophisticated mercantile empire of the Perushtarians, who have made a
commercial success of the cruel and ugly practice of
human slavery. Yes, I was perhaps lucky to have fallen
into the hands of the weird and inhuman insectoid
creatures . . . they at least were kinder to their

"possessions" than were most of my fellow human
beings to their unfortunate slaves!

Rolling along in the wain, I pondered my situation, which was dismal enough. Out of the frying pan
into the fire, as the old apothegm has it. From captivity in Tharkol, to slavery among the Yathoon.
And where were Darloona and Ergon and the others? Had they survived the crash of the balloon
safely, or were they injured or even dead? It was tor-
ment to me, not knowing whether my beloved Princess lived, and not knowing her whereabouts.

The clan who held me captive reminded me in
many ways of Koja's clan. But I doubted that they
were the same. There was no reason why they should
be, for the mighty Yathoon nation was divided into
many clans, all strikingly similar. The Yathoon culture, such as it is, achieved its present level of social
development uncountable millennia ago, and froze in
stasis. Little has happened to change their ways in all
those ages. In this respect, as in their physical being,
they closely resemble the social insects—ants, bees, ter-
mites—who achieved a social organization on Earth
millions of years ago, and have developed no further
in all that time.

Koja's clan roamed the Plains below the jungle
country of the Grand Kumala. That was something
like three hundred and fifty *korads* (or about 2450
miles) from here. I knew the warrior clans of the
Yathoon Horde held hereditary tribal rights to certain clearly demarcated areas of the Great Plains.
Thus it was unlikely, if not actually impossible, that
this should be the same clan as that which took me
prisoner when first I arrived on Callisto nearly two
years ago.

That night we made camp, drawing the wains and
chariots into a great double circle, patrolled along the
outer perimeter by mounted guards, while the retinue of each chieftain staked out a portion of the inner
area for his uses and erected his tent. The ordinary
warriors slept on the bare ground, rolled in hides and

furry cloaks, while the chieftains slept within the tents, surrounded by the hoard of jackdaw's treasure. That included me, of course.

They fed me a thin, watery gruel and, leashed to an underling named Hooka, I was led out into the open to perform my natural functions before being bedded down for the night. This was humiliating but, again, not without an element of humor: I was to be walked on a leash to relieve myself, for all the world like some rich Park Avenue matron's pet poodle!

On the way back to my quarters I made an important discovery. A voice hailed me: a voice that I recognized!

"Jandar!"

I looked up in astonishment.

"Ergon, you old rascal! So you survived the wreck of the balloon!"

"Aye—not without a share of bumps and bruises, though. So you got away from the *ghastozar* ..."

"Yes; how is my Princess?"

"Unharmed but furious at this captivity. She will be delighted to learn you are safe and near. Princess Zamara will not be so pleased, however. She had been enjoying herself by tormenting your lady with dire, gloating predictions of your grisly death in the jaws of the *ghastozar*. Little Glypto says—"

But then Hooka was upon me, jerking at my leash savagely.

"No talk!" he grated, jerking me along.

I exchanged a wave of the hand with Ergon before he, too, was jerked along by the Yathoon who was walking him as well.

I was so weary from the exertions of the previous night that I slept soundly, with no dreams. True, I was a prisoner with small hope of freedom. But at least my Princess was safe and unharmed, if an *amatar* like myself.

At least we were all together again.

Chapter 11

A Glimpse of Freedom

Although I was bedded down in the central tent wherein slept my owner, Borak, I was not permitted to sleep in his company. A nest of furs in a far corner was set aside for me, with several folding partitions separating the master from his store of treasures.

My nest was comfortable enough, I suppose, although I shared it with a curiously misshapen tree root, the polished skull of a jungle *deltagar*, an egg-shaped stone banded with stripes of some yellow mineral, a sack of broken glass and bright pebbles, among which were about a dozen diamonds the size of walnuts, and a jumble and clutter of odds and ends of every description.

This junk I shoved aside, making a bed for myself up against the outer tent wall.

I had been asleep for some hours, as I later judged the time, when suddnely awakened by a hand laid lightly on my mouth. I shot bolt upright, tingling in every nerve, until I recognized the scrawny, cheerfully grinning little rogue who had so unexpectedly roused me from my slumbers.

"*Glypto?* How came you here?" I whispered hoarsely.

He held up a bit of copper wire, then pointed to the slave ring about my ankle, chained to a tent pole.

"Glypto the *chanthan* is the master of many arts," the bony little rascal chortled, "and not the least among them is a certain skill at the opening of locks. Few are the locks that can withstand the skills of Glypto, the son of Glypto, the grandson of—"

"Spare me the genealogical reminiscences," I groaned protestingly. "My Princess—is she unharmed? Ergon—"

"We are treated well, as prized possessions of a chieftain known as Gorpak, whose scout party chanced upon us shortly after the flying thing came down with many bruising and bone-crushing bumps from its giddy travels through the skies of—"

I cut this flow of pointless verbosity short with a grim gesture.

"Have you some message for me, or is this just a social visit?"

"Oh, yes my master! The lord Ergon—who has laid hands of cruel violence upon my person, as you shall hear—the lord Ergon bade me inquire of you whether or not we should attempt an escape during the hours of darkness. I can open all our locks, for my skills are such that no lock devised by human ingenuity can for very long withstand the subtle probings, and the clever pokings, of Glypto's cunning and oh-so-sensitive fingers—"

"Do you know where the *thaptors* are penned?"

"Alas, but no! It is pitch-black outside, and the two great moons, formerly aloft, have since sunken—"

"Can you spare me a bit of that wire sufficient for me to free myself from the lock?"

He nodded and worked it back and forth until it broke in two. I secreted the length of wire within the lining of my tunic.

"Very well, then. Tell Ergon that when we camp tomorrow night we should both try to find out where the beasts are penned; then, when we are given our nightly walk for sanitary purposes, whichever of you four I see I will say something like 'It's a nice night for a stroll,' which is the signal to await the middle of the night—say about this present hour—then we shall separately free ourselves and meet at the pens for an attempted break. Do you understand all that?"

He nodded eagerly.

"About the mid of night—'A nice night for a stroll'—meet at the *thaptor* pens—aye, my master! Glypto will pass the word to our companions in misfortune!"

"Very well, then. Now get you gone, back the way you came, and be wary of the sentinels . . . good luck!"

He melted into the shadows, then darted back to thrust something into my grip.

"A small gift selected from the hoard of Gorpak, which may come in handy, master!"

Then he wormed his way under the edge of the tent and was gone in the night.

I looked down at the object he had thrust into my grasp.

It was a slim scabbard of green leather stitched with gold wire. In it was thrust a long dirk or poignard of blue steel, with a slender, tapering blade that was a deadly needle of razor-edged steel, with a hilt studded with rough gems.

I chuckled with surprise and tucked the thing beneath my tunic.

No telling when a weapon might come in handy!

That day we covered many weary, endless leagues of grassy plain under a sky of burning golden vapor.

As nearly as I could judge our direction on a world in which the sun does neither rise in the east nor set in the west, the Horde was moving northward in a succession of slow stages. Wherever they were going, they were certainly in no particular hurry to get there, for the vast procession dawdled along with frequent stops.

The reason for this was, quite simply, that they were actually going nowhere at all. The Yathoon Horde had left the Secret Valley in the Black Mountains at a certain season of the Thanatorian year, in order to follow the vast migrant herds of the *vanth*. I have already explained how, at this time of year, the *vanth* migrate across the Great Plains to graze and breed among the foothills of the mountain country to the south. The Yathoon were engaged upon a vast, year-long hunting expedition which would gather and preserve game meat to be taken back to their females and their young in the Valley of Sargol.

The Yathoon are the greatest hunters I have ever encountered; the greatest, in fact, that I have ever even heard of. In part their supremacy in this art is due to their innate nature: they are emotionless, coldly logical, and their thinking processes are thoroughly alien to ours. They are, therefore, capable of cool, infinite patience. A Yathoon hunter will track his game unswervingly, untiringly, for weeks on end whereas we more volatile humans will quickly become bored and turn to something else. Then again, the Yathoon are uniquely outfitted by nature for the role of huntsmen because of their peculiar sensory apparatus.

I don't know enough about the scientific study of the insect life-forms to be able to say with any certainty that this is true of terrene arthropods, but the Thanatorian variety have radically different senses from we humans. They see differently, with superb perception of distance and a heightened sensitivity to color. My friend Koja has told me that he and his kind can perceive twenty-seven different and clearly distinct colors in that segment of the visual spectrum we humans lump together crudely under the single heading of "red." As well, the insectoids have a greater sensitivity to odor than do we. They can sense the presence of game on the wind long before they can see it, and with their amazing ability to perceive color they can see through nature's every attempt at camouflage.

The Yathoon have another sense which they call *hamouph* and which is completely unknown to us. It seems to be the dimly telepathic ability to detect the nearness of highly developed living organisms, excluding vegetation and small, insignificant kinds of game, combined with a sort of locator-ability. In pitch-black night, a Yathoon can somehow sense the nearness of a large animal, and can pinpoint his location with remarkable precision. I have come to the opinion that this sensory ability detects the vital aura of life-force exuded by larger animals.

The organs of the *hamouph*-sense seem to be the branching knobbed antennae which sprout from the forehead of the Yathoon, or from where the forehead would be if they had foreheads, which they do not. But even the Yathoon are uncertain as to this sensory apparatus, and the brow antennae seem also to be the site of another sensory organ as well. It seems odd to me that the same organ should serve two dissimilar senses, but such seems to be the case.

To preserve the meat they catch during these interminable hunting expeditions, the arthropods have domesticated a peculiar distant relative of theirs called the *xanga*. These are a species of wingless insects about the size of a full-grown dog, which resembles nothing so much as immense greenish gray bumblebees. The *xanga* are monosexual—if that's the word I want—and oviparous. That is to say, they are simultaneously masculine and feminine, or at least their bodies contain the rudimentary functions of both sexes. At certain seasons, one organ exudes a sperm-like secretion which fertilizes the ova-like cells developed in a neighboring organ. When the eggs have grown to a certain stage, the *xanga* hunt their prey—any smallish mammal or reptile which contains a sufficiency of fatty tissue—pounce upon it, and paralyze it with the venom contained in their stingers.

The eggs, thirty or forty to a breeding period, are then deposited in the stomach cavity of the helpless catch. The venom perfectly preserves the paralyzed catch and antibodies therein fight the process of decay and the proliferation of maggots. The fatty tissues are therefore ready to be devoured when the larvae of the *xanga* hatch within the flesh of the host.

Over countless ages the Yathoon have bred and domesticated these insects and a pack of the *xanga* accompany each hunting expedition so that the unique properties of their venom (which is harmless, once it has stabilized in the blood of the game) may preserve the meat they take. The ingenuity of the entire process is quite remarkable. In a terrene analogy, you might say the *xanga* venom acts as a sort of embalming fluid, inhibiting the decay of the meat, and it becomes neutralized in the blood so that the meat thus preserved may be eaten, either raw or cooked, without any ill effects.

Toward the *xanga* packs, the Yathoon have evolved a relationship that could be described as containing the rudiments of affection. There is no overt friendship in this relationship, as, for example, in that which exists between a human huntsman and his hunting dogs; but a crude proto-affection is there to be seen. Every huntsman will have his favorite among the *xanga* pack, and these are generally singled out by possession of a pet name. For example, Borak's favorite *xanga* was an immense brute he called "Durgo," which means something like "trustworthy."

How infinite are the abilities of intelligence to adapt to the environment . . . and to adapt the environment to the uses of intelligence!

The day-long hunt contained one bittersweet moment for me and my fellow *amatars*.

Toward midafternoon the shadow of a cloud moved across the forefront of the immense procession. I looked up . . . and my heart literally stopped beating in my breast.

For it was no cloud that had temporarily obscured the golden brilliance of the Thanatorian heaven.

It was an ungainly aerial contrivance, the work of human intelligence. The smoothly curved hull, ornamented with cupolas and balustrades and balconies and belvederes, floated to the measured pulse of fantastic jointed wings. Long banners unrolled slowly on the wind, fluttering from sternpost and pilothouse and masthead.

At an elevation of about one thousand feet, the amazing aerial contraption drifted overhead lazily, dwindling slowly away toward the eastern horizon.

It was the dream of Leonardo da Vinci material-
ized into reality by the brain of some unknown ge-
nius of Callisto . . . a true ornithopter, a bird-winged
flying ship!

I watched it sail lazily overhead and shrink slowly
into dark mote down east with an ache in my
throat.

So near . . . and yet so far away!

It was a symbol of freedom and safety and rescue—although, to the Yathoon, it represented a po-
tential menace. The chitinous arthropods drew in
their ranks, nocked their bows, prepared for attack
which did not come. To them, the Sky Pirates of Zanadar were still a living menace. Remote and inac-
cessible, set apart by their taciturnity from all intercourse with the human races which shared their
world, the Yathoon could not have known that the
Zanadarians had fallen and the Sky Pirates flew no
more upon the golden skies.

They could not have known that two of the flying
galleons had survived the destruction of the pirate
fleet, the *Xaxar* and the *Jalathadar*, now in the service of Shondakor.

With an ache in my heart, I watched the stately
galleon of the skies vanish gradually into the glare of
the east.

I did not need to see the golden banner that
floated from her stern to know her for the *Jalathadar*.

And I knew that among her crew were gallant
Lukor, stout Koja, young Tomar, Captain Haakon,
Prince Valkar, or other of our loyal friends, searching
the Great Plains for some sign of Darloona and Ergon and myself.

That night, as Hooka took me for my walk, I
spied Ergon being walked on a leash by a member of
Gorpak's retinue.

"Looks like a nice night for a stroll," I greeted
him, casually.

"It does that, in truth," replied Ergon.

"No talk!" grated Hooka, jerking my leash.

Chapter 12

Escape by Night

My dinner that night consisted of the usual wooden bowl of thin, watery gruel in which a few lumps of tough meat swam soggily. I devoured it mechanically, hardly bothering to taste it. Then I lay down in my nest among the treasures of Borak and awaited the hour of my escape.

Alas, the appearance of the *Jalathadar* in the skies had thrown the chieftains of the Horde into consternation. The Sky Pirates were seldom if ever known to raid this far south, because in this part of the world there were no cities, hence no merchant caravans, and hence nothing for the aerial buccaneers to raid. Borak and certain of the other chieftains, among them Gorpak, conferred late into the night, discussing this problem and examining and rejecting various schemes for the protection of the clan. I lay in the darkness of a far corner of the tent, shielded by partitions, counting the minutes and anxious to be gone.

True, I was not under observation and could perhaps have effected my escape then and there. But I deemed it too hazardous to do so while the tent was filled with Yathoon and the sentinels outside wide-awake and vigilant. So I composed myself, and tried to emulate the patience for which the arthropods were famous. Once the war council had ended, and the chieftains returned to their own quarters, and Borak himself fell asleep, the guards outside would relax their attention and I could make my break with every chance of success.

It grew later and later. Had Ergon and the others

already unlocked their shackles and crept to the *thaptor* pens? Were they waiting for me now, nervous, tense, fearful that my escape had been discovered? Had this cursed, poorly timed council ruined all our plans? Should I wait no longer for the appropriate time, but try to escape now, despite the danger of detection?

These questions seethed and swirled through my restless brain in a turmoil of confusion. It might well prove wise to delay our break until the next night, but I had already given the signal to Ergon, and it was too late to change the plans now.

At length, as the night wore on and the council remained undismissed, I resolved to try it, for better or for worse, for I could wait no longer. At any time the greater moons would begin to rise, followed by the gigantic, luminous orb of mighty Jupiter itself. Night would become as bright as day, and the chances of our making a successful escape from the encampment of the Horde would lessen dramatically.

I had surreptitiously practiced unlocking my slave collar with the aid of Glypto's bit of wire, and was confident that I could repeat the action in a trice. The locks were old and primitive, for the Yathoon do not work metals, and our shackles were plunder taken in a raid long ago, or so it seemed from their condition. I fished out the bit of wire Glypto had given me and inserted it into the lock, bending it this way and that to conform to the configuration of the lock's interior mechanism. A few moments later the lock sprang open with a click of metal which seemed startlingly loud to me, in my tense and jumpy mood.

I waited for an endless moment, holding my breath in suspense, to see if one of the Yathoon should come hither to investigate the sound, but this did not happen. Busy with their discussions, the arthropod chieftains had disregarded the odd noise as being merely one of the numberless small sounds of the night.

Loosening the gem-hilted dagger under my tunic, I

crept under the tent-flap and slithered into the
drainage ditch that ringed the tent of Borak.

And I froze motionless—

*Not ten feet from where I lay, one of the guards
of Borak's retinue stood, staring up at the sky, lean-
ing on a spear.*

Had the insect-man heard the rustle of the tent
fabric as I wormed under it, or the sound I had made,
slithering into the ditch? Heart thumping painfully,
mouth dry with tension, I lay motionless, waiting
for discovery.

The guard made a weird sight, staring up at the
sky where as yet only the smaller of the moons were
aloft. Dim shafts of multi-colored moonlight drew
highlights from the crablike shell of oily chitin which
encased his many-jointed, attenuated limbs. The faint
light flashed and glittered in the huge bulging eyes
of the uncanny creature. These eyes were swollen
globular patches made up of ink-black, mirror-bright
crystals. He looked like some fantastic statue of glim-
mering metal, some alien god or demon, as he stood
motionless, bathed in the dim flickering rays of the
colored moons.

Following his fixed, unswerving gaze, I stared aloft
but could see nothing in the skies above which might
have attracted his attention. Perhaps the nearness
of the *Jalathadar* had prompted the wary Borak to
warn the guards to be on the alert for a reappear-
ance of the flying ship.

At any rate I lay there, sweating, my guts knotted
with suspense, waiting for him to move, wondering
if he was going to stand there all night long.

Armed with the poignard Glypto had given me, I
suppose I could have leaped upon him and struck him
down. But the Yathoon are not easily slain with a
small blade, for their greasy chitin protects their vul-
nerable organs like a suit of armor, and surely the
sounds of the struggle as we thrashed about would
have been heard by the chieftains within the tent.

Then, all of a sudden, without the slightest warning, the guard turned and stalked away in the oppo-

site direction, leaving me limp and gasping with relief.

I scrambled to my feet and darted through the
trampled grasses to the inky shadow of the next
tent, and began making my way as swiftly and as
silently as I could to the collapsible pens where the
riding *thaptors* were housed.

I had carefully marked the location of the pens in
my mind when the Horde made camp earlier that
evening, memorizing landmarks so that I could easily
find them in the dark. Staying in the dense shadow
of the tents as much as I could, I unobtrusively made
my way through the camp. Half a dozen times I
stopped short and froze motionlessly in the shadow
as a Yathoon stalked by. Their huge multiple eyes
give them uncanny night vision, as they gather much
more light than do our organs of sight, but luckily
none of them saw me.

After an interminable time I managed to reach the
thaptor pens without being detected. The restive
bird-horses, uneasy and alarmed because of the unusual
activity in the camp, capered and trotted about, clash-
ing their parrot beaks and hissing like steam whistles.
In the uproar it seemed unlikely our getaway would
arouse attention.

Crouching in the thick grasses, I peered about,
searching for my friends. Had they managed to escape from the tents of Gorpak, or had they been
seized during the attempt?

A hand closed upon my foot and I almost jumped
out of my skin. Jerking around, I saw Ergon's froglike
face glowering at me from a nest hollowed in the
grasses.

"Jandar! We had almost given you up! I was about
to send Glypto to see what had become of you—"

"An unexpected war council in Borak's tent," I
whispered. "Occasioned by the appearance of the
Jalathadar this afternoon; did you see the ship as it
passed over our line of march?"

"I did," he grunted, "but failed to recognize it.

Your lady knew it at once, though."

"Where is she?"

He waved one hand. "Yonder, hiding by the water trough. Think you the *Jalathadar* will double back, giving us a chance to attract her attention?"

"There's a chance, at least. The fact that the Horde is camped here must have given Haakon cause to wonder if we might not have been taken prisoner. But we'll see—the problem now is to get out of the camp!"

"While waiting all this cursed time for you to come, I got five of the *thaptors* saddled up; they are tethered yonder by the trough. I have been devilishly worried that some *capok* would come ambling by and wonder why five beasts are still saddled up, but thus far nothing had chanced. Let us be gone from this cursed place before we are discovered . . ."

"I say amen to that," I replied in English, not bothering to translate. We wormed our way over to the trough, where my Princess lay, with Zamara near and little Glypto crouched trembling in the shadow of a bale of dried grasses. Exchanging urgent whispers, we climbed through the fence and mounted the saddled *thaptors*. They didn't like the idea of being mounted, and were unhappy about wearing saddles, and squawked and clacked their beaks and made quite an uproar. But luckily no one came to investigate the noise, as this is the usual behavior of *thaptors*, who have never been thoroughly domesticated anyway.

"Now how do we get out of here, Jandar?" Ergon growled.

"We unlatch the gates and ride out, leaving the pens open behind us," I said swiftly. "That way all the *thaptors* will bolt for freedom and the Yathoon will be too busy trying to round them up to notice us making our getaway. So, at least, we may hope!"

Unbelievably it was even simpler than it sounds. The moment I tripped the latch and the gates swung open, sixty tense, nervous, squawking, quarrelsome *thaptors* made a frantic burst for freedom. We merely rode along in the midst of the herd. With unerring accuracy they stampeded towards the perimeter of the camp, where rude earthworks had been built up to encircle and thus protect the encampment. Each time the Yathoon Horde makes camp they go through the routine of digging drainage ditches and setting up earthworks and erecting the pens, even if they only plan to spend the night before packing up and moving on. I believe, in this respect, they unknowingly emulate the ancient Roman legions.

Guards sprang up in front of us along the rampart, waving their arms and uttering harsh cries, trying to divert the stampede. But the wild *thaptors* refused to be diverted, and the guards vanished in a whirl of dust as the *thaptors* simply ran them down, trampling them underfoot. Then the earthworks rose before us, a rampart of packed earth about six feet high. The *thaptors* rose up and soared leaping over the ramparts in one smooth wave that was beautiful to see.

Before us stretched the endless plains, dim in the vague moonlight. The herd kept on straight in the direction in which it had first headed, although the herd began to thin out along the edges as groups of bird-horses detached themselves from the main body of the stampede, peeling off in all directions, obviously for the purpose of making their recapture more difficult.

We five managed to stay together, but with considerable difficulty, for our unruly mounts desired to veer off in this or that direction. To enforce discipline we freely used the little knobbed *olos.*

We flew along like the wind. Our beasts were wild with joy at freedom, and sped straight out into the shadowy plains with every ounce of speed their wiry, lean-muscled bodies possessed. They could not for very long manage to sustain this dizzying sprint, but while they could, they put the encampment behind them further and further with every instant of time that passed.

These were not the only *thaptors* the Horde owned, of course. There were many such pens scattered about the camp, each containing between twenty-five and two hundred beasts, depending on the rank and importance of the clan chieftain to whom each pen belonged, and to the size of his retinue. But by the time the Yathoon saddled up and rode out into the plains to start trying to round up the runaways, we should be long gone.

Or so we hoped.

I leaned over the stiff ruff of bristling feathers my *thaptor* wore for a mane, feeling exultation rise in me, heady in my veins like rare champagne. The taste of freedom can make you drunk with joy, if you have not sampled the beverage for some time. Ahead of me, riding like the wind, my Princess turned to laugh joyously, her magnificent eyes smiling into mine. For the millionth time I gave thanks to whatever fate had made so glorious a woman mine.

By contrast with Darloona's wild excitement, the Princess of Tharkol clung fearfully to her steed, her face white with terror. The events of the last couple of days must have seemed like a nightmare to Zamara, for seldom could the proud and pampered Princess of Tharkol have been used with such rudeness.

We had snatched her from her bed, bundled her bound and gagged into her own balloon, carried her off for a wild ride through the skies, endangered her with pterodactyls, crashed her unceremoniously into the plains, gotten her captured and enslaved by a wandering army of savage and inhuman nomads, and now thrust her into the midst of a wild and giddy stampede of maddened *thaptors!*

The divine right of kings—or whatever silly philosophy she believed governed her incontrovertible right to do what she alone wished—must have become severely bruised in the recent succession of events. To say nothing of a tender and overinflated royal ego.

When one is carried off in the night by one's own

captives, it must be difficult to sustain the belief in one's divinely decreed destiny to rule the world!

As for Glypto, the little rogue was also white with terror and retaining his place astride the galloping *thaptor* with the very greatest difficulty imaginable. In fact, I expected the little rascal to go flying at any moment, from the way he was bouncing about in his saddle. But he wrapped both arms around the arched neck of his *thaptor* and clung on with every atom of strength his wiry little body could muster. But he was tough, the little bantam, and displayed unsuspected reserves of what I can only describe as guts. Life in the gutters and alleys of Tharkol thins out the weaklings early on, I surmised: to survive at all, he must have been tough and resilient and adaptable.

Glypto had survived. And he might even survive this wild, nightmarish gallop through the windy dark. But—from the way he was bouncing up and down in his saddle—I presumed he would not feel like sitting down for some days to come.

The headlong pace of our steeds slowed now as the beasts lost their wind. They began to stumble and stagger, gasping for breath, froth dribbling from the gaping beaks.

The larger moons soared up, one by one, over the edges of the world, flooding the plains with beautiful colored light.

We were lost and alone and unarmed in an unknown world.

But at least we had regained our freedom.

Book Four

SHAPHUR OF SORABA

Chapter 13

Lost on the Great Plains

After a time our beasts became exhausted and could no longer sustain their speed. We permitted them to come to a halt, and dismounted stiffly from the saddles. No sign of pursuit was either visible or audible, and, as we had ridden a considerable distance from the Yathoon encampment, we assumed it unlikely that any of the nomads were on our trail. Doubtless they had their hands too full of the problem of rounding up as many of the escaping *thaptors* as they could to bother about us. If indeed our own escape had been noticed, which was not likely.

Although we were by now completely lost on the Great Plains, without food or provisions or much in the way of weapons, save for the two poignards Glypto had discovered amid the hoard of Gorpak, one of which I had and Ergon the other, we were unafraid. In fact, we faced the unknown future with great confidence: we were free, we were together again, and we had a fighting chance of finding our way home.

In fact, our chance was better than that, for we knew our friends were searching for us, as an aerial galleon such as the *Jalathadar* can cover an immense tract of land very swiftly.

We camped where we were. None of us had extra clothing or anything in the way of bedding, but the night was warm and the grasses were deep and we were exhausted from the strain and exertion of our escape and our wild ride over the plains, and knew we could sleep soundly. Luckily we had all been fed earlier in the evening, and thus did not suffer from hunger, although I for one could certainly have done with a drink of water, and so, doubtless could my companions, especially the women.

Of the two women, Darloona was a tower of strength but Zamara, predictably enough, was a continuous headache. My Princess was too delighted to be free again to bother much about bedding down amidst the grasses, and viewed the entire experience with a boyish delight as an unexpected adventure. Her high spirits and enthusiasm were an inspiration to us all, and I loved her all the more for her humor, bravery, and cheerful willingness to endure discomfort.

The self-styled Empress of Callisto, on the other hand, could not stop complaining. She raved and ranted on about the affront to her imperial rank, cursed the Yathoon as unfeeling savages, and even had the nerve to protest about the undignified manner in which we had arranged our escape. The rest of us paid little attention to her fuming display of temperament, and Ergon, sprawled out beside me listening to her curse and complain, grinned sourly.

"It has been like this ever since Gorpak found us in the wreckage of the balloon," he grunted. "She was astounded that the Yathoon warriors did not know who she was, or *what* she was, I should say. And it enraged her that they paid not the slightest attention to her protestations that she was the Empress of the world and that by taking her prisoner, they tempted the wrath of the Lords of Gordrimator, whose anointed vicar on Thanator she was."

He chuckled. "The ultimate insult, which left her gasping and in tears, was that Gorpak's warriors chained her together with Glypto and your lady and myself. For an Empress to be chained with common slaves was a shock to her self-esteem from which she has not yet recovered!"

I laughed. "We shall have to find some way of disabusing her of this notion that she is the darling of the gods. The fact of the matter is, quite simply, that she has been deluded by Ang Chan."

"The little yellow dwarf who contrived our cap
ture in the woods? What part does he play in thes
mad dreams of world conquest?"

"He is a Kuurian from a far land on the other sid
of the planet," I informed him. "I have met his kin
before. One of his brethren, a clever little devil wh
called himself Ool, had connived himself into a pos
tion of high authority among the Chac Yuul. Th
Kuurians are Mind Wizards; they have the peculia
ability to read men's minds, and they know what yo
are thinking as well as you do yourself. And now
have reason to suspect that they have also the powe
to intrude into your mind and plant illusior
there—such as the white *vanth* Darloona and I pu
sued into the woods that time—the *vanth* whic
you could not even see, for the very good reason th
it was Darloona and I they desired to capture, whil
they cared nothing about you."

"A strange story, Jandar," Ergon mused, rubbin
his jaw with one huge, scarred hand. "It sounds lik
magic to me, and magic is something that I hav
never bothered to believe in. Had anyone else tol
me such a story, I would have thought him a fool or
madman or a liar. But I know you too well by no
to think you qualify for any of those titles."

Darloona, curled sleepily near us, spoke up. "Jand
speaks the truth, Ergon. He fought and slew this O
in the Pits of Shondakor, and the little yellow ma
thinking himself invulnerable because he could rea
Jandar's mind and knew where he would thrust h
sword next, unwisely bragged aloud of the secr
plans of the Kuurians, whom, it seems, work behin
the scenes to influence and direct other nations, fc
some cunning and mysterious purpose of their ow
And we did indeed see a white *vanth*, that day."

Zamara had permitted her ravings to subside, as
became obvious none of us was listening, and ha
heard our discussion. Now she came over to where w
sprawled in nests of trampled grass. She was still
remarkably beautiful young woman, though her fine
was by now reduced to rags and her hair had n

en tended for days. Her brilliant eyes flashed and
r lovely face flamed with indignation and fury.

"What madness is this you talk of, fools? Ang
ian is the wisest of my councillors and a holy man,
e veritable mouthpiece and oracle of the gods! You
ll him a cunning and unscrupulous rogue, plotting
eason—deluding *me?* But this is madness! The
ords of Gordrimator in Person have descended to
iil my future glory and to assure me of Their un-
iling support and miraculous assistance in paving
y way to the Throne of Shondakor—"

"Princess, is it not true that this Ang Chan pos-
sses a mysterious power to influence the thoughts of
hers, and to make their eyes see what his own
ind wills? Was it not by this power that he made
see the illusion of the white *vanth*, in order to
re us into the woods where you were waiting to
rry us off?"

She snorted indignantly at my words.

"Of course! He has the power to work holy mira-
es—a power given him by the Lords of Gordrima-
r in order to serve their ends—nothing more!"

"Perhaps not. But consider . . . if he could make us
e a *vanth* where Ergon saw nothing . . . could he
t also have made you see this visitation from the
ds you speak of?"

"That was a holy miracle! A blessed vision!"

"Is it not at least possible that the vision was in-
iced in your mind by the cunning of Ang Chan?" I
gued persuasively. "You must admit that it is at
ist *possible* that our interpretation of this vision
correct?"

"I—I—I admit nothing! You speak blasphemy
ainst the Lords—and treason against your Em-
ess!" she stammered.

Darloona eyed her with cool amusement.

"I suspect that the Princess of Tharkol is trying
sperately to persuade *herself*, not us, that her
iions were holy truth," she observed. "And I fur-
er suspect her vehemence stems from her own in-
r doubts, rather from any irrationalities in our ver-
n of these events."

Zamara glared at her in a paroxysm of furious outrage. Her breasts rose and fell as she panted, and her superb eyes flashed dangerously.

"You—*dare?*" she hissed.

Darloona shrugged. "Not having been a witness to these visions myself, I cannot be certain of their veracity," she said calmly. "But I would, I think, tend to be suspicious of anyone who tells me he has received miracles and visions from the gods. If there be any gods at all, in truth they dwell far away and seldom have anything much to do with human affairs—as witness the wars and tyrants and injustices that flourish unchecked, or, rather, are checked only by human effort and courage and dedication, if they are checked at all. And I would tend to be doubly suspicious of any miraculous visitations that tell you what you most want to hear: that you are destined for glory and greatness and deserve to rule the world. That sounds like wishful thinking, you know."

Words failed Zamara at hearing these unutterable blasphemies spoken in so calm and reasonable a tone of voice. Speechless, she stamped her little foot in rage.

"There—there is no arguing with one who refuses to believe!" she cried in vexation.

"There is also no arguing with one who insists on believing in the incredible against all reason and commonsense," Darloona smiled.

The Empress turned on her heel and went fuming off, to throw herself down for the night in a nest of grasses. She had removed herself as far apart from we unbelieving mortals as she could, without getting too far away for us to spring to her protection should danger arise.

We laughed and joked a little between us, then gradually let weariness overtake us and drifted, one by one, to sleep. The *thaptors* grazed on the thick grasses, tethered near to where we were bedded down, their reins securely knotted in the roots of nearby bushes.

We slept soundly, dreamlessly, and woke with dawn refreshed.

* * *

Refreshed, but furiously hungry and afire with thirst!
There was nothing we could do to assuage either hunger or thirst for the moment, however, so we simply
ignored them as best we could, keeping our spirits
high and facing the pangs of our empty bellies with
as much fortitude as we could muster.

Darloona remained cheerful and uncomplaining,
and not one word of peevish ill-temper escaped her
lips. Zamara, in striking contrast, wept and whined
and whimpered.

I would have thought her convictions of her divinely-ordained destiny would have sustained her in
the face of such trials and discomforts, but such, it
seemed, was not the case.

We mounted and rode into the plains. Ergon was
in the fore, his keen eyes searching the meadowlands.

When I asked him if it was game he was on the
alert for, he grinned and advised me he was keeping
on the lookout for a *jinko*. When I blandly asked
him what kind of a creature a *jinko* might be, he
goggled at me with astonishment, then shrugged
good-humoredly.

"I keep forgetting that you are not native to
Thanator," he shrugged.

"Then permit me to remind you of my ignorance,
and to inquire again into the peculiarities of the
jinko," I smiled. "Let us hope that they are good to
eat and easy to kill, for we have only two daggers between us and I am famished."

"It is not a beast at all, it's a plant," he explained. "A most curious plant, however, in that it
possesses the power of locomotion, otherwise denied
most forms of vegetation."

"A walking plant, eh?" I repeated, wonderingly.
"Well, the wonders of Thanator never cease to
amaze me. I trust this perambulating vegetation is,
at least, edible."

He then expanded on the unique qualities of the
jinko, a plant superbly designed by nature to subsist
in desert places, but often found amidst the plains,

especially in such parts of the plains which are de-void of rivers, ponds, or lakes. The *jinko*, it seems, is drawn to the nearness of subterranean water sources by some occult sense. Having found such, the *jinko* sends down its mobile rootlets to suck up the water, which it stores in hollow, bladder-like leaves, and upon which it sustains itself during further perambu-lations about the landscape in search of yet other sources of liquid nourishment.

The arrangement sounded most novel to me, but it was not, after all, very much more peculiar than that of the so-called "air plant" of my native world, which roosts in trees and drinks sustenance from the atmosphere alone, without recourse to the soil which is the common food source of most plants.

We rode on across the Great Plains, strung out in a wide front, each of us keeping an eye open for the elusive and invaluable *jinko* without which, I as-sumed, death from thirst and starvation was to be our lot. Zamara complained, loudly and continuously, about her hunger and thirst, but sulkily refused to as-sist in the hunt. It occurred to me to suggest that, as the chosen darling of the gods, she might expect miraculous relief for the asking; but that otherwise, unless she helped search for the *jinko*, she would have no claim in the partaking of its fluids.

She cursed me sulphurously, but began searching for the *jinko* as soon as she thought I was not watching her. I exchanged a grin with Darloona.

"Another week of this and, between us, we'll make a human being out of her," the Princess chuckled.

Chapter 14

The Tree that Walks like a Man

Before we had been riding for more than a couple of hours, Ergon raised an exultant shout and whirled his *thaptor* off in the direction I assumed to be north. He rode straight for a large, conical-shaped tree that towered above the plains to the height of some fifteen feet or so.

Riding up to where he had halted near the peculiar-looking tree, I called out to him. "This is a *jinko?* You didn't tell me they were as large as this—I was watching for something more like a bush."

"Such they usually resemble," he grinned happily, "but this is the grandfather of all *jinkos!*"

He climbed down off the back of his bird-horse, and made a warning gesture of caution.

"Don't talk too loudly or move too swiftly," he advised, "or you will scare it off."

I elevated my eyebrows.

"Scare it off? You mean the thing has—*intelligence?*" I asked incredulously. He shrugged indifferently.

"I know not whether it be true cognition, or mere brute instinct," he growled in a low voice, "but they are somehow sensitive to the nearness of warm-blooded creatures, and any abrupt movement in their immediate vicinity may alarm them into flight. And, while they are generally ponderous and slow of movement, I have known instances when it was necessary to gallop after one for the better part of half a *korad* before you got near enough to snatch a drink of water."

Glypto, Darloona, and Zamara had ridden up to

where we stood by this time. Wiser than I in the techniques of stalking the wary *jinko*, they dismounted slowly and formed a great ring about the tree, slowly moving in from all sides simultaneously.

The *jinko*, by the way, resembled an overgrown bush more than a tree, on closer inspection. That is, it seemed to have no central trunk from which the branches grew, but was a thicket of intertangled twigs, each about as big around as my forearm. The base of these twigs was a tangled network, like a great pad, which rested on the surface of the plain. Below this pad hairy rootlets of sinuous and snaky prehensile ability wormed deeply into the ground—I knew this because even as I advanced slowly upon the tree from my side of the circle, one wriggling rootlet came sucking up out of the soil and slithered inquir- ingly in my direction. In fact, it snuffled inquisitively about my feet like a wary and nearsighted dog!

The twigs extended about a dozen feet in all di- rections from the central mass, shaping the *jinko* into something like a squat cone. The twigs ended in swollen, purplish bladders rather like elephant ears, but much fatter because of the water stored within them. The fullest of the "leaves" were a good four or five inches thick and the larger of these must have contained nearly a gallon of water each.

The tree was aware of our presence now. The root- let which had been sniffing at my ankles, recoiled suddenly into a tight spiral, quivering and tense with alarm. Bristling long hairs or minor rootlets sprouted from the length of the wriggling, prehen- sile thing, and these vibrated, stiff with alarm.

I was reminded, uneasily, of a rattler, coiling and vibrant, about to strike. Snakes are unknown on Thanator, I believe, and Ergon, sensing my trepida- tion, advised me the tree was harmless.

Reaching up, we selected the fattest and largest of the bladder-leaves we could, and began cutting them off the branches with our knives. The tree jerked this way and that, trembling, trying to snatch its leaves from our grasp.

The leaves were quite easy to detach. Once you

snapped one loose, water dribbled from the end of the branch, which was hollow like a pipe or a garden hose; but the opening quickly swelled shut with an oozing, gummy substance. Watching this curious phenomenon, I suddenly realized that the "leaves" we were plucking were nothing like leaves at all, but were more like bubbles or balloons! For the gummy sap which oozed from the end of one branch from which I had just snapped off a "leaf," now swelled into a reddish bubble from the water pressure, and as I watched, it began slowly to expand into another elephant-ear-shaped bladder. As the gummy stuff stretched and dried, it turned purple.

When we had harvested enough bladders of water, Ergon bade us stand clear of the tree. Once it perceived itself to be no longer ringed about, the *jinko* nervously detached itself from the earth, and began scuttling off to the west, squirming along on its wriggling rootlets, swaying from side to side in a most amusing fashion.

Picking up its stride, it rocketed off across the plains and dwindled from sight. When last seen, I would say it was running much faster than a man.

Thanator—world of wonders!

You drink from the bladder-leaves by cutting or tearing a slit about two inches wide in the purplish flesh, tilting this aperture towards your mouth, and squeezing the bladder gently, causing the water to squirt into your mouth—and all over your face, if you fail to aim it properly.

The water was pure, clear, cold, and indescribably delicious.

Ergon made a fire with dry grasses and cut two of the empty bladders into long strips, toasting these in the blaze. They sizzled like steaks roasting on charcoal, giving off a steamy, spicy odor that was not exactly meatlike, but not quite vegetable either. When the strips were done sufficiently, we feasted on them. The purplish flesh, now crisp and brown, had a stringy, fibrous consistency like good lean beef, but a succulent, mealy taste like hot tortillas.

Anyway, they were tasty and filling. Even Zamara devoured them hungrily, failed to complain at the primitive nature of the feast, and carefully licked up every crumb from her lips with a small, pointed pink tongue.

We had drained dry, then cooked and eaten, only two of the *jinko* leaves. As we had plucked about seventeen before permitting the walking tree to scuttle away about its business, we had provisions of food and drink sufficient to last us for several days.

Resting awhile, seeing that the *thaptors* satisfied their thirst, we mounted and rode on, refreshed and filled.

Now the only pressing and immediate problem which we faced was that we were lost.

This was a problem that took some thought to solve.

We had been in the plains to the east of Shondakor when first taken prisoner. The balloon had flown us yet farther east, to the city of Tharkol. In making our escape from Tharkol by balloon, we had been carried, as far as we could determine, due south to be brought down midway between Tharkol and the Black Mountains. Midway between the city and the mountains we had fallen captive to the Yathoon Horde.

But which way had the Yathoon nomads taken us—east or west? I believed we had traveled due west during our captivity in the Horde, and should therefore be south of Shondakor. But Ergon was of the opinion that we had been headed north, and might by now be on a line between Shondakor and Tharkol.

It was a pretty problem, indeed. If we went in the direction I suggested, and if Ergon proved correct in his estimate of our present location, we should end up near the city of Soraba on the shores of Corund Laj, the Greater Sea. And that would make us farther from Shondakor than before!

The damnable part of it all was that we could not

be sure. This was due to the peculiarities of Thanator itself. The sun is merely the brightest of stars in
these skies. In fact, only rarely can you discern its
position in the heavens at all, due to the weird layer
of translucent golden vapor which blankets the Jungle Moon high in its upper atmosphere. Daylight on
Callisto is caused by some mysterious fluorescent effect in this golden vapor, which causes it to blaze
into illumination. But this happens all at once,
throughout the entire sky.

On Earth, things are so much simpler. The sun
rises in the east, and that's all there is to it! Once
you know this fact, you can figure out your direction
during any daylight hour. But not so on Thanator.
And here they have yet to invent the compass!

At length we resolved our differences, arrived at a
compromise, and struck off in a direction that we
generally agreed would in time bring us within eye-
shot of Shondakor.

We crossed the plains by slow, easy stages, with
frequent stops for rest and nourishment. Had it been
just Ergon and I alone, we could have made much
better time, because we would have increased the
pace, driving both ourselves and our *thaptors* mer-
cilessly.

But we had the women to think of, and scrawny
little Glypto. Half-starved most of his miserable life,
the little guttersnipe lacked the stamina of a warrior. So we catered to him and the women, nor did
we treat the little rogue harshly, demanding he keep
up with us. He was no enemy, but a friend, and I
must admit that I felt just a bit guilty at forcing
him to endure these adventures. He had been
brought along with us by a combination of accident
and mistake, and it seemed a bit unfair. I must say,
all things considered, he was a more amiable and use-
ful companion than his Queen, who alternately raged
or wept, whimpered or cursed. He was good-natured,
comical, and quick to help. He amused Darloona
with his quips and antics, and he delighted in tormenting glum Ergon.

He delighted in mimicking Ergon's goggle-eyed glower and froggish grimace, and skillfully parodied the bandy-legged Perushtarian's rolling gait, which always reminded me of a sailor's. Ergon suffered Glypto's clowning in indignant, grim-jawed silence, but, when stung to the quick, made to cuff the capering little thief. If any of those heavy-handed blows had actually landed, Glypto would have clowned no more—nor, for that matter, would he have stirred from a hospital bed for a fortnight.

But he seemed to know by sheer instinct when Ergon had taken enough, and whenever his antics had goaded the bald-headed Perushtarian to the brink of rage, the smirking little rapscallion slackened his play and turned to other trickery, leaving Ergon to huff and puff as his temper slowly subsided.

There was a considerable element of play in this, as if it were almost a game shared between them. I have a feeling Ergon, in his dour, grumpy way, rather liked the chipper, droll little guttersnipe, and that little Glypto admired Ergon for his strength, valor, determination, and dogged loyalty. The unspoken, almost unavowed, friendship or comradeship which grew between the two very dissimilar men was touching, in a way. Neither admitted to any fondness for the other: Ergon snorted, and called him "gutter-scrapings," "garbage-picker," and like terms of disrespect; Glypto, on the other hand, employed his nimble wits to invent a variety of amusingly apt, if impolite, titles for Ergon. Of these the one which amused me most was "Sir Boiled-Frog," a deft allusion to Ergon's scarlet hide, bald head, bowlegs and froglike mouth.

Our supply of *jinko* bladders lasted us six days without scrimping.

On the seventh day we encountered, and raided, a second *jinko*. Our second was nowhere near the size of our first, which had been indeed, as Ergon termed it, the "grandfather of all *jinkos*." This one, by comparison, was only a niece or nephew. Moreover, we took it on the wing, so to speak: it was not rooted, but roaming free, and we had to chase the nimble-rooted little bush about three-quarters of a mile before we "winded" it sufficiently to bring it to a stop, which we effected by the simple process of surrounding it on *thaptor*-back, then dismounting to prune it of the larger of its bladders.

The poor thing trembled in terror all the while, but we did not denude it, picking only the larger of its leaves, before turning it loose to scamper off. The leaves were nowhere as large as the ones on the first *jinko*, but their water was no less fresh and cold, and the flesh of the bladders was, if anything, tenderer, juicier, and more succulent.

That was on the seventh day of our escape from the encampment of the Yathoon arthropods.

On the eighth day we saw the caravan.

Chapter 15

Taken by Surprise

The caravan consisted of about two hundred men and animals strung out in a long line that wound across the Great Plains for nearly half a mile. Teams were hitched to large covered wains which, with their four wheels, light construction, and felt coverings, bore a striking resemblance to the covered wagons which played such an important role in the opening up of the American West.

The drivers of these wains, and the scouts, guards, and outriders, who fanned across the plains in every direction, keeping a lookout for bandits or raiders, had the scarlet skin and bald heads and beardless faces of Perushtarians.

Leaving Glypto behind to stay with the women, Ergon and I went ahead to investigate the caravan and to form some estimate of the danger it presented to us, if any. We dismounted and wormed a way on our bellies to the crest of low hummocks from which we could view the extent of the caravan without being seen ourselves.

Ergon looked them over with a suspicious eye and a glum face.

"Sorabans," he grunted sourly.

"How can you tell?" I asked. He indicated the emblem which was emblazoned on the breasts of the riders' tunics and stenciled on the sides of the wains. It was also tattooed or perhaps branded on the upper chest of the *thaptors* where their feathers thinned out to a creamy fuzz. This symbol bore little relation to the earthly kinds of heraldry known to me. It was a complex design of flowing, intertwined arabesques and flowery tendrils.

"The emblem of the House of Iommon, a family of merchant princes very powerful in Soraba, who maintain a branch in Narouk," he growled. Ergon had been a slave in Narouk when first we had met, which explained how he was able to recognize the blazonry.

"Slavers?" I asked.

The Perushtarians have made of the breeding and training and selling of slaves a major industry and a fine art, and the last thing I wanted was to fall in with slavers. Not when we were this close to Shondakor, surely!

He shook his head, almost reluctantly.

"I have never heard that the Iommon interests extend to slavery," he said grudgingly. "They have a monopoly on sea trade between Soraba and Farz, and a share in the weaving and dyeing works in Glorious Perusht itself. They maintain a great fleet which plies the waters of the Corund Laj between the far-flung cities of the empire."

"Then we are in no danger of being enslaved by them?" I pressed. He shrugged.

"I should not think it likely. But it would be best if we permitted the caravan to pass us by without discovering our presence. We have been in enough trouble on this adventure, as it is. But there is something strange here. . . ."

"What is that?"

He shifted about to a more comfortable position in the grasses.

"I have never heard that the Iommon indulge in overland trading expeditions, and cannot imagine why they should bother to do so, since they enjoy a monopoly on sea trade. And I cannot help wondering where they have been, and where they are going. Their wains seem full of goods, their mounts travel-stained and covered with road dust; from this, I would assume that they have completed a successful trading venture and are en route home again."

It took a moment for this to sink in. As it did, and as I began to realize the implications of this, my heart sank.

"You mean you think they are heading for Soraba?" I asked, hollowly.

"I must assume so. And they could only have come from Tharkol, for there is no other city hereabouts."

"That means we *have* been traveling in the wrong direction, all this while!" I groaned.

He nodded, grimly. "I'm afraid so, Jandar."

"Then every hour we have ridden has only put more distance between us and Shondakor," I said in despair. He nodded again.

"I can only think so. We are headed due north, towards the shores of the Corund Laj, where the city of Soraba rises at the head of the Sorabanian peninsula." He nodded over his shoulder. "We should have been traveling in *that* direction, all this while!"

Just then we heard a despairing cry from behind us. We whirled to see mounted warriors cantering in a circle about Darloona, Glypto, and Zamara. They were caravan guards, from the emblems on their tunics, and they had ridden through the hillocks behind us, taking the women by surprise.

"Well, that blows it," I said grimly.

"Do not bother to translate, Jandar," Ergon grunted. "I think I can guess your meaning."

Since we were discovered, there was no point in trying to hide our position, and I had no wish to be parted from Darloona again. Ergon and I rose to our feet and hurried down the slope. One of the caravan guards spied our approach and cantered toward us.

He was a sulky-faced, grim-looking specimen, with a squat neck and a bullethead and surly, suspicious eyes, hard and mean and wary. A curved scimitar or cutlass hung at his girdle and in his left hand he carried a long war spear tufted with scarlet and black feathers, these being the heraldic colors of the House of Iommon.

The blade of this spear was pointed at our chests. We came to a halt and stood there empty-handed. My dagger was concealed beneath my tunic, as was Ergon's, or so I suppose.

Breathing heavily, Ergon stood in silence as the

guard cantered up to look us over.

"What have we here?" the guard growled, eyeing us up and down with curiosity.

"Harmless travelers," Ergon said quietly. "Why do you molest our women and our servant?"

"Why do you spy on the caravan of Lord Shaphur from a place of concealment?" the guard countered. Ergon had no ready answer for this and wisely held his tongue.

"We are no bandits, as you can see for yourself," I spoke up. "Two unarmed men, two women, and a servant pose no threat to your caravan. We were merely observing it from a place of safety, to see what it was and if it posed any threat to us. We are harmless travelers, bound for Shondakor."

His eyes were still wary and suspicious.

"Perhaps this is true," he grunted. "Then again, perhaps it is not. You are certainly a long way from the Golden City, and if that indeed be the goal of your journey, then you are taking a very roundabout way of getting there. Or so I gather from your tracks, which are heading in the wrong direction."

I was sweating, but tried not to show it.

"So we have just discovered from observing the direction in which your caravan seems to be traveling. I'm afraid we have been lost for some days, and, if your caravan is returning to Soraba, as we assume, then we have indeed strayed from our path. With your permission we will mount and be off."

"Not so fast," he growled, jabbing the spear in my direction. "I cannot permit you to pass on my own judgment; the Lord Shaphur himself will interrogate you and decide what should be done."

"That sinks it," I breathed to Ergon. And again I did not have to translate my terrestrial idiom for him to understand my meaning.

The master of the caravan—Lord Shaphur of the House of Iommon—was an immense, obese Soraban who rode at the head of the procession in a wain outfitted with great luxury and comfort. Cushions

were heaped into a cozy nest at one end of the lux-
uriously carpeted wagon, and therein the merchant
princeling sprawled at his ease, sipping a brandy-like
cordial called *quarra* and munching sweetmeats and
small pastries from a huge tray of glittering silver.

Shaphur of Soraba was one of the fattest men I
have ever met. He must have weighed close to three
hundred pounds, with his vast paunch and wobbling
jowls and several chins. He was dressed in the fantas-
tical manner affected by the Perushtarians of the
great houses, in a loose robe of silken stuff edged
with gold fringe, hung about with tassels, adorned
with sashes, and pinned with gaudy jeweled
brooches.

His robes were an incredible, eye-hurting clash of
colors—olive green, fuchsia, violet, canary, three
shades of pink, indigo, umber, and carnation. The
Perushtarians are a gaudy, mercantile people whose
civilization always reminds me of the Carthaginians
or Phoenicians of my own Earth—a nation of
shopkeepers, an empire of merchants. They have the
flashy Semitic bad taste of their terrestrial counter-
parts, and overdress to a fault.

This Shaphur was no fool, for all his appearance.
He looked to be a jolly fat man, beaming with good
humor, his paunch and chins and jowls quivering as
he chuckled at his own jests, but behind the fat, scarlet, merry face was a first-rate brain, and his eyes
were small, shrewd, cool, and intelligent.

He received us informally, squatting comfortably
in his nest, in the shade of a striped awning. Gauzy-
pantalooned slave girls knelt to either side of him,
making certain that his goblet was never empty and
his store of sweetmeats ever replenished. He looked
us up and down with clever, measuring eyes, all the
while stuffing himself with sugary pastries, which he
conveyed in a never-ending stream from platter to
gullet, shoving them in with both fat hands whose
greasy fingers were glittering with a profusion of
gems.

"What an oddly mixed traveling party, to be

sure!" he chuckled to himself in a husky, gasping voice, beaming all the while a broad, benign smile. I could not help noticing that this genial smirk did not extend as far as his eyes, which were cold and cunning and watchful.

"A Shondakorian lady of noble birth, quite obviously, accompanied by three Perushtarians from very different levels of society: a lovely and highborn lady of evident breeding, a burly rogue who seems suited to be a warrior or a gladiator, and a scrawny starveling from the gutters who would seem to have run afoul of the law—if I mistake me not the brand of thievery on the creature's brow—ho, ho!"

Glypto tugged a greasy forelock in an obsequious manner.

"Not so—not so at all, mighty and gracious lord! Glypto, the son of Glypto, the grandson of Glypto, at your Magnificence's service! A nobly born *chanthan*, alas, upon whom Fortune has declined to smile. . . ."

"Ah, so; of course," Shaphur chuckled. "The borders between *chark* and *chanthan* are narrow, at best, eh? Ho, ho! A merry rogue!"

Then the cold, thoughtful, measuring eyes turned upon myself.

"And you, my lad—what of you, eh? The strangest of all in this strangely mixed company of 'harmless travelers'!" he puffed in his light, wheezing voice. "What of you, eh? A stranger from a far-off land, no doubt; for never have I laid these tired old eyes on a lad with such peculiar coloration!"

"From a far-off land, even as you surmise, Lord Shaphur," I replied in even tones. "But, oddly mixed as we are, which is an accident of fortune and not of design, we are indeed harmless travelers as you say. And we would be on our way, if it please you. . . ."

"To Shondakor, I believe, if my outriders report correctly. Well, well! Yonder beautiful lady is indeed Shondakorian, if I may trust my weary old eyes to tell aright, but the rest of you . . . eh! What business can so many Perushtarians have in the Golden City?"

"Our business is our own, Shaphur!" a clear contralto voice slashed through the Soraban's labored, breathy tones. I groaned inwardly. For it was Zamara!

"*Lord* Shaphur, dear lady," he chuckled. "Let us observe the amenities, if you please. . . ."

"*Lord* Shaphur, I mean," Zamara said in a throttled voice.

"That's much better . . . your gracious ladyship would be, I believe, a Tharkolian, as would also be yonder starveling, as the both of you twain boast that hirsute adornment of pate denied to we coastal dwellers of the pure blood?"

"Tharkolians, yes . . . lord," Zamara said. She pronounced the word as if it strangled her to refer to another person by his title. It came to me then that perhaps Zamara possessed a modicum of good sense, after all; at least she had not yet loudly announced that she was Empress of all Callisto, and demanded that the smirking, oily fat man grovel at her feet.

"A pair of Tharkolians, a stranger from a far-off land a noble Shondakorian lady, and a Perushtarian—*from?*" he spoke sharply, stabbing a hard glance at sullen-faced Ergon.

"Narouk," grumbled Ergon unwillingly.

". . . Narouk . . . ah, yes, our sister city! Well, well. I understand you five so oddly ill-assorted traveling companions have become lost for some days past and strayed from your route . . . eh?"

"That is the truth, Lord Shaphur," I said evenly. "And, with your gracious permission, we should like to be on our way."

He flapped pudgy hands in horror at the suggestion.

"Oh, but, surely not until you have partaken of our famous Soraban hospitality!" he protested, wheezing. "Deprived of the civilized comforts during your unfortunate journey, reduced to devouring the crude and scarcely edible leafage of the elusive *jinko,* mounted on ill-trained and highly unsuitable steeds which bear, I perceive, tribal markings of the Yathoon barbarians . . . surely you must be my guests for a time, while you recover from your ordeal! Azaroosh, see that our guests are fed and made comfortable."

The guard so instructed made his salute and turned to guide us. Zamara sharply overrode this.

"You hold us captive, then?" she demanded imperiously.

Shaphur's fleshly face assumed a grimace of surprise.

"Ah, noble lady, you are in mistake! I, Shaphur of Soraba, your captor? Never! Say, rather . . . your gracious host, until such time, in the very near future, when you have recovered yourselves from the travails and discomforts of the journey . . . Azaroosh!"

And so we became the "guests" of Shaphur, merchant princeling of Soraba. Well, I suppose it could have been worse.

After all, Zamara had yet to tell him his guests included the regnant prince and princess of Shondakor, to say nothing of the divinely appointed Empress of the entire planet!

Chapter 16

A Little Soraban Hospitality

It could indeed have been worse. Our quarters were
in a large and commodious covered wagon whose interior was thickly and comfortably carpeted and
cushioned. It was not, of course, so richly decorated
as that sumptuous vehicle in which Lord Shaphur
traveled in state, but neither was it Spartan in its
furnishings. The Sorabans are more warlike and mon-
archical than the rest of the Perushtarian race, but
they do enjoy their creature comforts and have much
the same taste for luxurious accommodations as their
cousins of Farz and Narouk and Glorious Perusht itself.

Our wagon, like most of the larger wains, was
drawn by a huge, lumbering, heavy-footed draft animal called the *glymph*, which the Thanatorians prefer as a beast of burden to the light, wiry, temper-
mental *thaptor*. The difference between the two
beasts is much the same as that between the horse
and the ox back on Earth. *Glymphs*, however, don't
look much like oxen. They are about as large and fat
and heavy as rhinoceroses and look quite a bit like
the extinct prehistoric triceratops, with their flar-
ing neck shield of thick bone and several horns a-
dorning brow and snout. They are slate gray in
coloring, which hue fades to a dingy yellow in throat
and chest and belly, and for some inscrutable reason
of her own, Dame Nature has seen fit to ornament
the imposing creatures with tiger-stripes of an amazing shade of crimson.

Our *glymph* lumbered along, head down, waddling
with its heavy-footed stride, the reins held by our

driver, a glum, unspeaking Soraban with a long nose
and small, suspicious eyes called Laalmurak. He sat on
a sort of buckboard in the front of the wagon and
kept an eye on us, although an unobtrusive one. We
were neither bound nor shackled, as befitted our os-
tensible position in the caravan as guests of the man-
agement.

It wasn't bad, all things considered. We had luxurious sleeping-furs to curl up in and a plenitude of
plump, soft pillows, and none of these things were
exactly unwelcome to us, who had spent the past
seven days sleeping on the hard ground curled up in
the grass like so many rabbits. And Shaphur certainly
set a fine table for his "guests"!

I had almost forgotten what real food tasted like,
after a week of subsisting on broiled strips of *jinko*
bladder. As the caravan creaked and rumbled along,
we sampled a profusion of covered dishes which fitted neatly into small legged trays ideally designed
for eating while in motion. These contained a delicious, piping hot meat stew in steaming gravy, spiced
fish-cubes in cream sauce, hot meal-cakes sprinkled
with *sarowary* seed, marrow of *argang* in jelly, fresh
fruit, candied nuts, and beakers of a cool, green,
mint-flavored wine that rather resembled crème de
menthe.

We fell to with lusty appetites, emptying dish after dish with gusto. If *this* was Soraban hospitality,
thought I, where had it been all my life!

The only dish unfamiliar to me was the *argang*
marrow, a blackish, pungent paste that tasted
vaguely like caviar—although it had been so many
years since I had last partaken of that terrene delicacy, that I could not be certain my taste buds
weren't fooling me.

The *argang* was not a fish, despite its caviar-like
flavor, but a kind of crustacean found in the coastal
waters of the Corund Laj, and a delicacy greatly
prized by the gourmets of the Perushtarian empire—
which is really an oligarchy, by the way. For although the Perushtarian cities are leagued together

under the rule of a sovereign, his rule is a formality, and the wealthy merchant princes are the actual monarchs.

Ergon munched the caviar-like paste with a rare good humor. It had been a long time since he had left Narouk, and in all that time he had enjoyed few of the traditional delicacies of the Perushtarian art of cooking.

"Superb!" he mumbled, licking the last morsel off his thumb. "Do you know, Jandar, that the humble *argang* has a larger relative called the *harthak?* Only a half-spoonful of marrow may be extracted from the lowly *argang*, but it's larger relative, I have often thought, might yield a bushel of the stuff, were it not so damnably unfriendly!"

I chuckled. The *harthak*, I knew from conversations with Zastro, the old sage of the Ku Thad, were shellfish the size of a full-grown *deltagar*, and the most dreaded denizen of the deeps, save for the dragon-snake itself. The *harthak* were able to devour men alive, and did so without compunction, when the unwary diver came too close.

"I thought the *harthak* were prized for their enormous pearls, not for their contributions to the dinner table," Darloona smiled. Ergon nodded froggishly.

"Alas, 'tis so, my lady. But to each his own taste; for myself, I would rather fill my stomach with this delicious stuff than adorn my body with pearls. You cannot eat pearls, you know!"

"With a mouth the size of yours, my Lord Frog-Face, you could make a try!" quipped little Glypto, dodging an instant later as Ergon threw a spoon at him.

Replete, we napped for a while on the thick rugs, waking when night fell. Of all the times I have been held prisoner on Callisto, it seems to me that never have I been fed so splendidly. Even the luxurious cell we had shared in Zamara's palace had not offered a better cuisine. But I may be wrong: hunger always makes the best sauce!

"Why do you think this Soraban lordling has taken
us prisoner?" Darloona asked, nestled comfortably in
my arms, as we watched the many-colored moons of
Callisto rise one by one into the night sky, round
and ripe and richly colorful, like Japanese paper lan-
terns.

"I don't think we are exactly prisoners," I replied.
"There are our *thaptors*, tethered to the rear of the
wagon, and Shaphur has yet to put us in chains."

"But surely, Jandar, you did not believe his sly
words about being our 'gracious host'?" she asked incredulously. I shook my head.

"No, he was just amusing himself at our expense.
But I think he doesn't quite know what to make of
us, and is sort of keeping us on hand hoping to find
out more."

"Well, I hope Glypto doesn't talk too freely," she
said, with a slight shiver. "The poor, miserable little
creature has not the manly fortitude to endure much
pain, should Shaphur put him to the questioning
with any severity."

Only a half hour before we had been awakened
from our drowse when guards rode up to carry off the
little thief for further interrogations before the lord
of the caravan. He had been carried off, shrilly pro-
testing his innocence of any wrongdoing, in the
clutches of grinning guards. They had yet to bring
him back.

"There is no good worrying about it, my Princess,"
I said, hoping to calm her fears. "For there is nothing we can do about it, in any case."

Ergon grumped, clearing his throat.

"We could climb out of this thing, get on our *thaptors* and be off across the plains," he growled. "I still
have my dagger."

"I have mine, too," I said. "But how far do you
think we would get before the outriders were on our
necks?"

"Not far enough, I suppose," he grunted. "But it
irks me sorely, Jandar! Every minute we bump along
in this fancy cart, we are being carried further and

further away from Shondakor...."

"And nearer and nearer to Soraba," added Zamara, tartly.

"Why should that trouble you unduly, Princess?" I asked, glad that we were all on speaking terms again. Quite a bit of her high, imperious ways had been knocked out of her by our recent ordeals, captures, imprisonments, and escapes. These days, why, she was almost human at times.

"The Sorabans are no friends of mine," she said darkly. "My embassies demanded they surrender sovereignty to me last month. I had planned, by this time, to have included both Shondakor and Soraba within the borders of my empire. Now that my plans have gone awry, the rulers of Soraba are well on their guard."

"Which is why you did not announce your true identity to Shaphur when he questioned us, I suppose?" asked Darloona.

Zamara shrugged. "Of course. It would have been madness."

Ergon craned his head.

"Here comes that little guttersnipe, back again," he growled disgustedly. "I had thought that maybe we were getting rid of him this time," he swore.

Darloona grinned mischievously.

"Oh, Ergon, you great dissembler! You know you've really grown quite fond of the little scoundrel."

"I've grown *used* to him, if that's what you mean, my lady," he grumbled. "It was the silliest mistake I've ever made, pitching the squealing little runt in the balloon basket while Jandar was off fetching her high-and-mightiness, here."

Zamara bristled.

"Mind your tongue, slave! You refer to the Majesty of Tharkol! Were I back in my realm, I'd have your tongue slit for such insolence."

Unimpressed, Ergon voiced a rude snort.

"Doubtless you would, lady. But in Tharkol we are not, and right now we are fellow captives, and I'll say what I please."

Zamara subsided in a fuming silence while we turned to assist little Glypto to climb into the wagon. He was pale and whimpering with fear, and his one good eye, bright as a ferret's, rolled from side to side in terror. There was a purplish bruise on the side of his lank, unshaven jaw that had not been there previously, and another above his eye patch. He tumbled into the bottom of the wain, moaning piteously.

Ergon crouched over him, his ugly face anxious.

"Are you all right, little man? Did they beat you? Here—have some *quarra.*"

Glypto lapped up the potent brandy like a thirsty hound, and sank back gasping for breath.

"Did they beat poor Glypto?" he quavered. "Unmercifully! Unjustly! But good, brave Glypto the *chanthan* . . . told them nothing! Nothing at all! He remained faithful to the trust of his friends, although the great, cruel guards beat him with their terrible fists, and kicked him with their great heavy boots, and cursed him for a rogue and a thief and . . . and called him terrible names!"

Darloona shoved Ergon away, telling him to fetch a dampened cloth, and bent solicitously over the whimpering, moaning little rascal, who proved far less hurt than you would have thought from the way he carried on. He seemed to have been slapped a couple of times, and perhaps shaken up a bit, but he was otherwise unharmed.

Ergon joined me at the rear of the wain.

"Do you think he said anything unwise, Jandar?" he growled worriedly.

"What do *you* think?" I countered.

He grumbled unhappily.

"I think he'd probably sell his grandmother to be ground into sausages, to avoid a kick in the pants," he rumbled dolefully.

"I'm afraid I agree with your estimate of Glypto's fortitude," I said quietly. "The little fellow has many sterling qualities, but bravery in the face of punishment is not among them. We may, I think, assume that by now Shaphur is delightedly aware that his guests include at least three members of the royalty. Quite a coup for him, then, if he can manage to get us back to Soraba safely!"

"Then we must make certain he does not," he said grimly.

"Yes; but my former objection still holds," I reminded him. "We could doubtless get to our steeds unobserved, and perhaps even leave the caravan unseen, but the outriders would be onto us in no time, for, with all moons aloft, 'tis as bright as day on the plains at this hour."

"What we need is a diversion," he said thoughtfully. "Could we set the wagon afire?"

"With what? We have neither candle nor lantern."

"I still have my flint-and-steel," he said.

Then he stopped short.

For the caravan suddenly exploded into uproar and confusion! *Thaptors* bolted, or reared squealing—men yelled lustily—ahead of us somewhere a wain went crashing over on its side with a jolting thunder of splintering wood!

And a huge black shadow traversed the sky.

"A diversion, eh?" Ergon boomed heartily, staring skyward with an expression of slack-jawed amazement and huge joy.

I followed his gaze.

Above us, at the height of only a hundred feet, the *Jalathadar* serenely floated through the skies under the glory of the mighty moons.

Book Five

ANG CHAN OF KUUR

Chapter 17

An Unexpected Meeting

It was not so much a matter of attempting to escape, as it was of taking advantage of the occasion.
The sudden and unexpected arrival of the flying ship,
which hovered above us like some immense and mysterious apparition conjured out of thin air at the
whim of a playful magician, threw the orderly Soraban caravan into whirling chaos.

It is quite possible that the news of the destruction of the corsair fleet and of the overthrow of the
City in the Clouds had not yet reached the rather
remote and secluded seacoast cities of the red men.
There is little intercourse between the several city-
states of Thanator, and they are wary and suspicious
of each other, when not actually at war. And, as
well, hundreds of leagues of savage jungle or untamed
wilderness stretch between them, rendering travel
hazardous and infrequent.

At any rate, the Sorabans reacted as to the
presence of a powerful and ferocious enemy. The
heavy, lumbering *glymphs* waddled about squealing
in panic, toppling the wagons and smashing the
wains to splintering ruin as they stampeded. The
restive, unruly *thaptors* broke free and fled in every
direction. In a trice, the placid and well-ordered procession was a milling tangle of shrieking bird-horses,
plunging and rearing, dislodging their riders and
snapping with sharp wicked beaks at those who
strove to calm them. Bales, barrels, and bundles
went toppling to be trampled in the dirt underfoot
as guards dodged the beaks of the panic-stricken
thaptors and raced to block the escape of the rhinoc-
erine *glymphs*.

In such confusion—made doubly chaotic by the darkness and the many-colored blur of moonlight—escaping was easier than I could have asked. Our wagon came to an abrupt halt when the *glymph* hauling it started at the shadow of the ornithopter and backed into the traces, crushing the footboard. Our driver, Laalmurak, was pitched headlong from his perch and must have flung himself into a ditch, thinking the Sky Pirates were upon him, for we saw no more of him, nor did he interfere with our break.

Ergon and I sprang over the rearboard of the carriage and jumped down to the ground. The *thaptors* we had ridden out of the Yathoon encampment were tethered to the rearboard of the carriage, and, although they bucked and reared squealing, and lunged to snap at us, Ergon snatched up the little knobbed club that hung at the side of their saddles, and bludgeoned them into dazed submission.

Fortunately, the Lord Shaphur had seen no reason to unsaddle our mounts, which would have required finding sufficient space in one or another of the heavily-laden wains wherein to store the saddle gear, hence the beasts were ready for riding.

While Ergon, growling sulphurous oaths and whacking lustily at the heads of the brutes with the little club, held the bird-horses under control, I assisted Darloona and Zamara to dismount from the carriage. Little Glypto, still limping and whimpering from the effects of what he described as a cruel and merciless beating at the hands of Shaphur's brutal guards, climbed down painfully.

Within just a few minutes we were in the saddle and ready to go. Ergon slashed through the tethers with his dirk and we guided the beasts off the road and across the plains in the general direction of the *Jalathadar*, which had drifted slowly by overhead, and was engaged in wheeling about in a slow and stately maneuver, prior to making another pass over the length of the caravan whose progress its appearance had so precipitously disrupted.

These things we accomplished—miraculously—under the very noses of the red men of Soraba, not one of whom took the slightest notice of us in the act. They were busy chasing their runaway steeds or attempting to round up the lumbering *glymphs*. If any of them had sufficient leisure to spare us a glance, he likely saw Ergon—a bald-headed, red-skinned Perushtarian—and not the rest of us. For Ergon sat tall and erect, taking a prominent position for that very reason, while the rest of us bent low in the saddle and kept our faces hidden as best we could. But, so complete was the milling confusion into which the procession had degenerated, that I doubt we were noticed at all.

Thus, by a happy accident which might well prove our salvation, we bade the Lord Shaphur a hasty adieu, and left the hospitality of Soraba behind us.

We headed out into the moonlit plains at a right angle to the road the caravan had been following, which was only a beaten track through the grasslands of northern Haratha, and not a paven way.

If the caravan had been headed in a northerly direction, as was our surmise, then our route was due west. We were riding, then, more or less in the general direction of Shondakor, although of course the Golden City of the Ku Thad lay many *korads* distant. With luck still on our side, as we assumed, it seemed likely we should not have to traverse the leagues of meadowland bestride our steeds, but should ride, or rather fly, in comfort and safety.

But that still remained to be seen.

The problem was, quite simply, one of finding a way to attract the attention of our friends aboard the *Jalathadar*.

The mighty galleon of the skies was slowly cruising at about thrice the speed of a racing *thaptor*, and now rode at a modest elevation of about eighty feet aloft. As the great airship swung about for another leisurely pass over the caravan, many eyes probed through the moonlit darkness from above, narrowly surveying the Perushtarian caravan. I have no doubt our friends aloft were pausing to investigate the peculiar circumstance of finding a merchant caravan in this part of the country where, as I have intimated earlier in this narrative, there is little reason for any caravan to be.

Our only hope of rescue, then, lay in somehow catching the eye of one of the alert watchers from above.

But how?

The elusive moonlight was brilliant but confusing to the sight, for several of the many moons of giant Jupiter were aloft—and the web of light and shadow they cast was tricky to the eye. The shifting moonbeams—lime green, silvery azure, dim red, pale golden—made it curiously difficult to perceive details or to see colors.

Of course, this is usually the case on virtually any world at night, or, at least, on any world of my experience. On Earth I have noticed that it is nearly impossible to make out any colors even by the light of a full moon, the only exception to this rule being scarlet or crimson, which take on a darkly purple tinge by the gray-silver luminance of Earth's only satellite.

This being so, we thought it likely we might hope to attract the attention of our friends aloft by doing something distinctly curious and odd.

So we rode out boldly into the plains, directly away from the caravan, keeping well together in a clump for added visibility, and making not the slightest attempt to conceal our flight. The caravan guards, we knew, were still too busy rounding up their beasts and organizing a hasty defense for the expected battle against the aerial corsairs (as they doubtless suspected our craft to be one of the flying buccaneers of Zanadar), to bother about us, or even to have noticed as yet that we were missing. Hence our failure to attempt to conceal our flight from the caravan was not likely to bring about immediate recapture or even pursuit by the Perushtarian warriors.

It was, however, very likely to catch the eye of

someone aboard the *Jalathadar*, and to arouse his curiosity. He would understand the Sorabans mistook
his ship for a Zanadarian corsair; but he would naturally expect the members of the caravan to seek
their security in numbers, rather than to go racing
off across the plains as we were doing.

Such, at least, was our estimate. And such, indeed,
was our only hope at present.

As we rode out of direct view of the caravan, I sat
straighter in the saddle and held my head high. My
yellow hair, which is of a coloration utterly unique
among the many nations of the Jungle Moon, has
saved my life on more than one occasion. And if any
detail of our appearance were likely to attract the
attention of our comrades aloft, it would be the
bright, straw-yellow locks bequeathed me by my
Danish mother.

Or so I hoped . . .

Once we were out of sight of the confused mass of
roiling men and beasts and overturned wagons that
had been the merchant caravan of Lord Shaphur, we
boldly strove to call attention to ourselves.

As we rode, we shouted and windmilled our arms,
staring up as the galleon cruised by, silent as a ghost,
enormous as a cloud, directly above us—

And halted!

Someone above had seen us; someone, perhaps, had
recognized us. Or had they?

A moment later rope ladders came tumbling over
the side and we raised a ragged cheer. Swiftly we
dismounted, Ergon and I tumbling out of the saddle,
with Darloona and Zamara and little Glypto not far
behind.

The vessel hung directly above us, blotting out the
moons: a vast, fantastic winged shape of blackness.
Ergon sprang up and seized the lower rung of the
nearer ladder, then reached down to give a hand to
one of the women. I leaped into the air to catch the
bottom rung of another ladder, and gave poor stiff
and sore Glypto a hand.

Then we clambered up the swaying ladders slowly,

hand over hand. Below us the *thaptors*, delighted at
the unexpected prospect of freedom, cantered
blithely off across the grasslands, anxious to get away
from their proximity to the hovering aerial monster.
I wished I had taken the time to remove their bridles,
reins, and saddles, so they could enjoy their newfound freedom unencumbered by the accouterments
of enforced domesticity, but the rescue of my Princess was of uttermost importance in my mind, and
doubtless, with their sharp saw-toothed beaks, the
unruly gryphon-like creatures would manage to free
themselves of the straps and saddles before long.

Forgetting the *thaptors*, I grinned at the prospect of a safe and comfortable flight back to Shondakor in style. A bit of luck had come our way at last, I
thought to myself.

Above me I could see Ergon bestraddling the rail,
and heard him cry out as he gained the deck. The
wind of this height snatched his words away so that
I was unable to hear what it was he had called out.
Undoubtedly, he had hailed with delight one of our
dear friends on the deck—Koja or Valkar or that little gamecock, Lukor.

Then Darloona climbed over the rail, helped by
one from the deck whose face I could not make out,
as he was only a black silhouette against the moons.
She too voiced a sharp cry of delight, I assumed, before vanishing from my sight.

Below me little Glypto clung dizzily to the slats
of the rope ladder, squealing in terror at the height,
shrieking as the ladder swayed to and fro in the
wind of the great jointed vans that beat up and
down in slow booming strokes, maintaining the vessel's height.

I grinned at his panicky distress. Soon enough the
wizened little thief would be wined and dined in the
captain's salon, and when we returned to the Golden
City tomorrow, Darloona and I would find the
means of repaying the little fellow's adventures on
our behalf with a cozy sinecure. True, the little man
had been an unwilling accomplice in our escape, but

we should make all his perils and sufferings up to him, I was sure. He would doubtless feel well repayed for his discomforts and dangers by being given a commission as a tax collector!

Grinning at the thought, I climbed the last few yards and reached up, took hold of the rail, and started to haul myself up.

A dark shape blotted out the moons above me as it stood at the rail.

I looked up smiling . . . and felt the world fall apart under me.

For I looked into the bland, smiling face of Ang Chan.

Chapter 18

The Secret of Zamara

The evil, slitted eyes of the yellow dwarf gleamed into mine as I clung to the rail, frozen with shock and utter astonishment. He smiled benignly at my expression; the smile, however, did not extend as far as his eyes, which remained cold, wise, and cunning.

So complete was the amazement which gripped me that for a moment I was incapable of thought or action. I was possessed with a feeling of horror, which numbed my brain and paralyzed my limbs. How came the yellow devil aboard the *Jalathadar*—had the Tharkolians somehow tricked or overpowered or captured the galleon of the skies? And if so, what had become of our friends who must have been aboard the craft at the time of its seizure? Gallant Lukor and loyal Koja and bold Valkar and the others would surely have resisted the boarding party with all the valor and courage they possessed. Were they themselves captives of the yellow fiend from mystic Kuur? Were they perhaps—slain?

While these frightening conjectures whirled through my dizzy head, burly arms seized me and dragged me over the rail to stand me on the deck of the *Jalathadar*. The midship deck swarmed with the brawny, truculent warriors of Tharkol; nowhere could I see Shondakorian captives. Across from me, held helpless in the grip of many hands, Ergon glowered wrathfully, and Darloona cast me a beseeching glance, white-faced, from fear-haunted eyes. My comrades had been seized and gagged as they reached the deck rail, and I now realized that their cries had been of astonishment and horror, not of delight, as I had at first assumed.

The Tharkolian warriors trussed my hands securely behind my back, relieved me of my dagger, which I still wore concealed in the breast of my tunic, and sent me stumbling across the swaying deck to stand with my friends.

The irony was heartbreaking: an instant before we had stood on the brink of freedom. And now we were again thrust into the shackles of captivity.

Zamara alone stood free and unbound. She bestrode the deck like a conqueress, black locks flying on the winds, her lovely face arrogant and proud, flushed with triumph, laughing at our discomfiture. At last the tables were turned, and she was the victor again, the captress, and we were once again the captives, subject to her lightest whim.

But how had this amazing reversal of events come about—and how could the Tharkolians possibly have captured the *Jalathadar?* The great ornithopter could not land, must remain ever aloft. How then could it possibly have been boarded and taken? Surely, not through such flimsy and capricious a device as the balloons whereby we had been first captured and had later effected our escape from Tharkol?

Ang Chan greeted his empress effusively.

"How fortunate, Royal Lady, that the Prince of Shondakor chanced to bare his head to the rays of the many moons! Even the shifting hues of the moonlight could not conceal from our eyes the un-likely yellow of his hirsute adornment!"

She laughed recklessly.

"And how fortunate, Ang Chan, that the *Arkonna* reached its long-delayed completion in time to rescue your Empress from the clutches of our enemies. You are to be congratulated!"

He bowed obsequiously. "It was a matter of prime importance, which I pressed with all urgency. Luckily the vessel was so nearly finished that it was only a question of days. . . ."

These cryptic words made no impression on my dazed mind. *Arkonna* is the Thanatorian word for "high king" or "emperor" with a feminine ending: it meant, then, "empress." But what did these puzzling

remarks mean? Had the captors of the *Jalathadar*
rechristened the vessel already?

While these questions revolved through my brain I
was so positioned by those who held me that I faced
the prow of the vessel. Within my sight was the
door which led down to the private quarters of the
captain. The door was familiar to me, of course, for I
had passed through it many times. But now, gazing
at it unthinkingly, it came to my attention that
something was strangely wrong with its appearance.
Just what it was that seemed wrong I could not at
first identify.

And then it came to me. The blazon painted on
the panel of the door was not what it should have
been!

The royal blazon of Shondakor, you see, consists of
a shield of gold charged with a winged crown above
crossed swords. After we had seized the vessel many
months ago, we had painted out the blazon of its
original Zanadarian corsair captain, replacing it
with the royal emblem of the Golden City.

But the emblem was different, now: it was a crimson field which bore eight black crowns, a blazon
which was unfamiliar to me. Then it came to me
where I had seen that strange coat of arms before—
on the armorial plaques and banners which had
adorned the great hall of Zamara's palace in Tharkol!

The eight crowns must represent the eight cities
of this hemisphere of Thanator. The blazon, then,
was of the world empire whereof Zamara in her madness dreamed.

Which meant . . . *we were not aboard the Jalathadar at all, but on a newly built Tharkolian vessel!*

The thought electrified me; I stiffened in the
grasp of my captors, looking about me with a startled gaze. Now that the veils had been stripped from
my eyes, so to speak, I noticed things that had
eluded my attention previously. There were subtle
differences in the design of the deckhouse, in the
sculptured adornment of the balustrade; minor inno-
vations in details of the rigging and the equipment
stored or housed on this deck.

Ang Chan caught my eye. Bland amusement gleamed in his slitted eyes. The yellow dwarf, with his uncanny mind-reading powers, must have sensed the tenor of my thoughts, for he came over to where we stood and laughed.

"The Prince of Shondakor has surmised the truth, I see," he purred. "Doubtless the noble Jandar was of the opinion that the ambitions of the Empress Zamara were the delusions of a deranged mentality! How could a single city such as Tharkol, for all the might and valor of her legions, conquer the seven cities of the world? Vast distances, impenetrable jungles, savage wildernesses and uncharted seas separate the cities of Thanator the one from the other; to dream of welding these far-flung realms into a single empire must have seemed to the noble Jandar a mad dream and nothing more. . . . But now you perceive a frightening truth, which places the imperial ambitions of Tharkol within the borders of possibility, am I not correct?"

"You are," I said, striving for calmness. "For I perceive that the city of Tharkol has discovered, or has been given, the lost secrets of constructing the aerial warships of Zanadar."

Ergon grunted and Darloona stiffened with astonishment at my words, but the Mind Wizard only smiled and made an ironic little bow as if saluting my powers of deduction.

"Quite so," he said silkily. "Doubtless the Prince of Shondakor assumed the science of building the ornithoptors lost with the destruction of the Sky Pirates. Such is, however, not the truth. For the Lords of Gordrimator have revealed unto the chosen vessel of their will, the future Empress of all Callisto, the techniques perfected by the Zanadarian savants. And you stand aboard the *Arkonna*, the prototype of the flying navy of Tharkol, which has been under construction for the past three months, together with her sister ship, the *Conqueress*, which will shortly reach completion."

Zamara interrupted Ang Chan abruptly. I got the impression that she had wished to announce these triumphs before us herself, and resented his assuming the role of spokesman.

"Enough, yellow dog! Guards—remove the prisoners to the cabins aft and see them securely imprisoned. Use them not with unwonted severity, however, for they are valuable to us and their persons are not to endure mistreatment. Later, we shall interrogate them at our leisure."

Ang Chan bowed to her peremptory wishes and we were led away.

Our cabin was commodious and not uncomfortable, if Spartan in the bareness of its furnishings. We were at the rear of the flying ship, stationed directly over the rudder assembly, and the creak of cordage and the boom of wind in the rudder were deafening, however. The rudder, like that on the *Jalathadar* and her sister ship, the *Xaxar,* was a towering structure of ribbed vans rather like an antique Chinese fan, by which the vessel was steered. A row of barred windows looked out on the rudder assembly and gave us fugitive glimpses of the night-drowned landscape which glided steadily beneath our keel.

We discussed the rather gloomy situation into which chance or fate had now thrust us. Darloona was incredulous over the fact that the warlike Tharkolians possessed an airship, and apprehensive concerning the implications of this fact on the future security of Shondakor.

"How could Zamara have rediscovered the Zanadarian secrets?" she wondered, as we shared a meager breakfast served us by surly, watchful, and unspeaking guards.

"What is more curious, my lady," grunted Ergon sourly, "is how the Tharkolians came by supplies of the lifting gas which makes the sky ships airworthy. When we touched off the gas mines in the White Mountains, destroying the city of the Sky Pirates, I thought we had eliminated the only source of the mysterious vapor known to exist."

I set down my goblet. "That may well have been the truth, Ergon," I said. "But at that time we dis-

covered that the lifting gas wherewith the hollow
hulls of the ornithopters are charged was explosive
and flammable. On my own world we have a similar
gas which was also once used in the construction of
flying vessels and which is also explosive and flammable. We call it *hydrogen*. And our savants possess
knowledge of a technique whereby the elements
which constitute ordinary water can be divided by
use of a force we call *electricity*. By this manner, it is
easy enough to produce as much hydrogen as may be
wanted. However, I had not thought the several
races of Thanator possessed any knowledge of electricity. Perhaps I have underestimated the cunning
and cleverness of the Mind Wizards of Kuur in this
respect, as in others."

Darloona sat frowning slightly, nibbling absently
on a bit of fruit. "What worries me most," she con-
fessed, "is that if the Tharkolians have one sky ship
already in operation, and a second near completion,
and an entire fleet of others under construction, poor
Zamara's mad dreams of empire may yet attain reality. That will be a grim day for Shondakor, and a
grim day for all of the cities of Thanator. . . ."

Little Glypto huddled woefully on one of the
bunks, clutching his bony shanks. "Far better, my
masters, had we stayed with the Lord Shaphur!" he
whimpered.

I shook my head wearily. "It is all my fault," I
said. "How foolish of me to have mistaken the *Arkonna* for the *Jalathadar!* It simply never occurred to
me that the flying ship could be any other than the
Jalathadar. The *Xaxar*, which Zantor commands, is
somewhat smaller and higher in the aft-section. . . ."

Darloona slipped her hand in mine.

"The fault is not yours, beloved," she said. "We had
none of us the slightest reason to guess the Tharkolians knew the secrets of building the ornithopters.
Your mistake was perfectly natural; indeed, I made
it, too."

"What baffles me," Ergon growled, "is how the
Queen learned the building of such ships. The levitating vapor is but one of the secret techniques. How

did she learn of the molded-paper construction which makes the vessels light in weight yet strong? The Zanadarians pressed wet paper sheets over plaster forms and baked them, once they had been impregnated with glue. The lamination process alone is one that involves many secrets . . . and, of course, we cannot accept the lady's mad belief that these secrets were imparted to her by the Lords of Gordrimator. The gods may or may not be omniscient; but it is a fact of history that they have seldom, if ever, meddled in the affairs of men."

"I'll wager it was the doing of Ang Chan," I said grimly. "You will remember the positioning of his apartments in the palace of Tharkol? He was only separated from our own suite by a wall, near enough to read our minds as we slept and learn the secrets of the defense of Shondakor and the disposition of troops. But when Glypto led us through the secret passage hollowed within the walls, we discovered that the private apartments of the Queen also lay nearby . . . near enough, I'll wager, for his telepathic powers to feed images and visions into her brain as she slept. For surely if one has the power to eavesdrop on the minds of men, one has also the power to subtly insinuate thoughts and pictures into that mind. The cunning of this yellow devil is extraordinary. He has deluded the Queen of Tharkol into thinking that she is an instrument of destiny, chosen by the gods to conquer the world. And all the time she is nothing more than an instrument of the Mind Wizards of Kuur, who secretly plot the conquest of Thanator for their own hidden and inscrutable ends—'"

"You lie, you blaspheming Shondakorian dog!"

Out of nowhere a shrill voice, choked with wrath, knifed across my ruminations.

We started, upsetting the wine goblets. For the voice seemed to come from the empty air itself.

In the next instant the mystery was solved. For a hidden panel in the wall clicked open and Zamara stood before us, flanked by two powerful warriors whose naked blades were leveled at our breasts.

Chapter 19

Truth and Trickery

Never before had I seen the would-be Empress of Callisto in such a towering rage. Her handsome features were distorted into a staring mask of fury. Her brilliant eyes blazed with wrath and the emotion which flamed up within her lithe and supple figure was so furious that she trembled in its violence. Almost I despaired of my life in that instant. So maniacal was her rage, that in the next moment I thought to hear her command her guards to bury their steel in our hearts.

"These are the same vile slanders and vicious insinuations wherewith you strove to beguile me from the truth of my revelations, that first night we spent on the Great Plains after making our escape from the encampment of the stinking *capoks!*"* she spat. "You strove to turn me against the gods then, and you scheme to do so now."

"How could we be other than sincere in our statements, since we could not have known you were listening to our conversation from a place of concealment?" asked Darloona, reasonably.

The sheer commonsense of her words took Zamara aback. She blinked, fumbling for words. At her side, the glowering guards fingered the hilts of their weapons, waiting for the word to sheathe their blades in our breasts. I could feel the sweat break out on my forearms and my brow.

---

* A rude racial euphemism frequently employed on Thanator to indicate disrespect for the Yathoon arthropods. It is an impolite colloquialism which may be translated as "bugs."—L.C.

Into the tension of this emotion-charged scene, the calm reasoning of Darloona interposed itself between our helplessness and Zamara's fiery wrath. Indeed, looking back on the scene, I am convinced that it was the words which Darloona now spoke which served to save our lives. For she alone remained cool and collected in the heat of the moment.

"Sister," she said, "for we are fellow rulers, sisters in a sense, sharing between us neighboring thrones, believe me, it is *you* who blaspheme here, although you know it not."

Zamara, her right hand lifted in an imperious gesture, as if about to signal her guards to fall upon us, checked the gesture. It was as much the serene reasonableness of Darloona's tone, as well as the surprising import of her words, which served to check the rage of the Tharkolian princess.

Her furious gaze turned on Darloona, who regarded her with calm, unfrightened eyes, an expression of sadness on her features.

"*I—?*" Zamara gasped in a strangled voice.

My Princess nodded sorrowfully.

"Yes, Zamara, although it pains me to speak of it thusly. O, listen to me, royal sister! We are both women, born to be fooled and victimized by men, for all our regal authority and majesty of birth! We are both queens, are we not—Both born to the throne, both born to rule, you and I. Surely by now you must have learned how cunning, unscrupulous, and ambitious men flock about a throne, flattering and lying and betraying one another, eager to grasp as much of our own power as their scheming wiles can win. Is it not so?"

Wordlessly, Zamara nodded.

"Very well! Then hearken to our words, which you overheard from your place of concealment while spying on us—and understand that we could not have known that you were listening, and thus we spoke our minds, and gave voice to the sincere opinions of our hearts. Is this not obvious?"

Again, the logic of her words, and the calm fear-
lessness in her voice and composure, wrung a reluctant
nod from the infuriated empress.

"Very well, then. Zamara, royal sister, we believe—*we know*—that you have been cunningly and
systematically deluded and deceived by this sly yellow dog who has wormed his way into your highest
councils. He is not the first of his kind we have encountered among the councils of our enemies. When
the Prince Jandar, my mate, entered in disguise the
legions of the Chac Yuul which had seized and con-
quered my realm, he found a cunning Kuurian named
Ool occupying a high position of great power and influence. And this Ool had won an office of great and
subtle power over the superstitious minds of the
simple Black Legion barbarians by a trumpery cult of
his own creation. A false god he called Hoom was
the method he employed. And under his sway the
Chac Yuul won the realm of Shondakor from my people—*even as, under the influence of his fellow countryman, Ang Chan, you are now embarked on an attempt to conquer not only Shondakor, but all of the
cities of Thanator.*"

Zamara stared at Darloona, the color draining
from her scarlet visage. The madness and the fury
had faded from her magnificent eyes, to be replaced
by thoughtfulness.

"Something of these matters regarding the priest-
ling, Ool, and his hold over the former Warlord of
the Chac Yuul my spies have informed me," she muttered slowly.

Darloona rose to confront her.

"Think, royal sister! Never before in all the history of warfare did it occur to the mercenaries of the
Black Legion to conquer a city or to seize a throne.
And in the councils of the Black Legion dwelt a yellow-skinned foreigner from Kuur, squatting like a cunning spider at the center of his web! Never before in
all the history of mighty Tharkol did it occur to any
of your ancestors to attempt the conquest of the
world. And in your own councils dwells yet another

yellow-skinned foreigner of Kuur, spinning his plots and subtle intrigues! Can you not see the similarities between these events?"

Zamara eyed her distrustfully, saying nothing. But the expression in her features, and the look in her eyes, conveyed the fact that she was indeed listening and thinking—however reluctantly.

"The Lords of Gordrimator have visited me in my dreams," she said sullenly, after a little silence.

"Was it the gods, or was it the weird power of Ang Chan, interfering with your sleeping mind?" Darloona pressed her. "If you overheard our conversation, you will recall our discussing how Ool the Uncanny influenced the Black Legion warriors— through the cult of the god Hoom. Is it not reasonable to guess that this second Kuurian used the same method to influence you—the gods? And furthermore, Zamara, can you doubt the ability of Ang Chan to insinuate his own pictures or thoughts into your brain? You know that he is perfectly capable of performing this feat, because you were present when he did it to us, causing us to see the illusion of a white *vanth*, which led us into your trap. If his mental power could persuade us that we saw a white *vanth* where there was really no such beast, certainly those same powers could persuade you that you had received the visitation of the gods."

Zamara wavered indecisively, biting her lower lip with vexation. She was an intelligent girl, with an excellent mind. And I could see that Darloona's calm and reasonable arguments had made some impression on her, but how much of an impression it was impossible to ascertain.

At this point, I spoke up.

"Queen Zamara, in my homeland the philosophers hold to an axiom which says: when confronted by two alternate solutions to a question, the less fantastic of the two is most likely to be the true answer. Think! The Lords of Gordrimator may or may not exist; and if they do exist, they may or may not influence the actions of men; and if they do influence

men upon occasion, they may or may not have influenced you. But the abilities of Ang Chan certainly do
exist. We have all experienced his powers in action.
There is no question of his uncanny ability to tamper
with our very thoughts. Now: faced with the question of whether the unknown and inscrutable Lords
of Gordrimator have visited your dreams, or whether
it was merely the known and genuine power of Ang
Chan which made you think so, and remembering the
axiom I have just mentioned, which of the two
assertions is more likely to be true?"

We waited. Would her intelligence win out over
her delusions, or would human nature conquer the
dictates of reason and commonsense? For Zamara very
desperately wanted to believe her visions and voices
and gods were true. She possessed a vaulting ambition; it would be very difficult for her to turn her
back on the luring dreams which promised crowns
and glory and conquest. What monarch would not
wish to believe he is the instrument of the gods, the
chosen favorite of fortune, the darling of destiny? To
believe what you want to believe is only human
nature.

And Zamara was very human.

But reason won out over avarice and vainglory.

Her features strained and pale, her eyes mutinous,
her voice hesitant and reluctant, she said: "It is more
likely to assume . . . that Ang Chan has used his
powers to delude me. . . ."

At that moment we heard the guards beyond the
door of our cabin ring their spears against the deck
in salute.

And one of them called out: "Make way for the
Lord Councillor Ang Chan!"

The next moment a key grated in our lock.

We were about to receive a second visitor!

The yellow dwarf paused in the open doorway to
look us over with keen, wary eyes. Two guards
flanked him, eyeing us truculently. We sat about the
folding table which was littered with the remnants

of our morning meal. I held a silver winecup in my
hand as if I had just emptied it. Zamara and her
guards were nowhere in sight; we had, by sheer urgency, begged her to trust us for the moment, and
thrust her and her warriors back into their place of
concealment, regaining our own seats a bare fraction
of a second before the door opened, showing us the
bright morning sky and the smiling person of Ang
Chan. He entered, bowing amiably.

"This unworthy person thought it wise to visit his
guests and ascertain their comfort and, ah, the measure of security they enjoy, before our arrival at Tharkol necessitates his attentions," he said in a suave,
good-humored voice.

There was no reason Ang Chan should not be in a
good humor, as he held the upper hand. Perhaps
even the winning hand, although that was yet to be
seen.

I came directly to the point.

"You are one of the Mind Wizards of Kuur, are you
not, my lord Ang Chan? I knew a countryman of
yours, one Ool, called 'the Uncanny' by the simple
warriors of the Black Legion he had bewildered and
awed by his telepathic powers. Do you know him?"

He surveyed me with amused, twinkling eyes.

"The mission of the worthy and resourceful Ool
was known to this humble person, but, alas, not the
worthy Ool himself. I believe the honorable and
inestimable Ool met his untimely demise at the hands
of a certain terrene adventurer who calls himself
Jandar of Callisto."

I nodded. "That is true, Ang Chan. Tell me, are
you of Kuur born with your abilities to manipulate
and eavesdrop upon the minds of others, or is it a
skill acquired through training?"

"Your inquisitiveness may lamentably shorten your
duration of existence, Prince Jandar," he observed.
But good humor was irrepressible. "An inclination towards the art is innate in our race; proficiency in the
art, however, is the result of stimulus by certain rare
drugs upon the proper brain centers, employed in

. accord with certain disciplines of mind, body, and spirit. Why do you bother to inquire into the minor attainments of this insignificant person?"

"Because I am interested to find out how you worked this trick of fooling the Queen of Tharkol into thinking herself visited by the gods," I said boldly.

He drew in his breath, his eyes suddenly going cold and opaque. Then he relaxed with a small, chilly smile.

"You are insolent," he observed. "And that is unwise. When one holds the power of life or death over you, it is imprudent to provoke him so."

"Then *you* are in control of events here, and not your Queen?" I demanded hotly. "I surmised as much!"

He smiled thinly. "Zamara is the beloved of her gods and leaves many of her merely mundane affairs to this lowly person," he admitted, suavely.

"Gods of the same sort as Hoom, the idol of the Chac Yuul—a thing of dead, empty stone?" I pressed.

"In dealing with the lesser races, we of Kuur oft have found it auspicious to play upon their superstitions," he said.

"Then, like me, you are a skeptic?"

He shrugged casually. "The gods may, after all, exist in one sense of the word or another. But if they do, they seldom bother with mortal men. . . ."

"And, with your telepathic powers, you find it easy to make superstitious men believe they have experienced visions of the gods—when it suits your purpose to do so."

"All too simple," he laughed. "The lesser races are eager to be convinced of their own importance in the eyes of their gods."

"As it was easy for you to convince Zamara of her divinely-ordained destiny, because she hungered to believe therein?"

"The ambitions of royalty render it easy for us to gain ascendance over them by telling them what they most desire to hear," he said blandly. "Their own convictions of superiority shape them as a tool to our uses. But it is not of these matters I would speak—"

His voice broke off suddenly and his face paled. Slitted eyes bulging with horror, he sucked in his breath and spat aloud one word.

"Tricked!"

The rasp of steel sounded behind us.

We turned. Zamara stood there in the secret opening, her face hard and cold, her eyes ablaze with deadly anger, a naked dagger clenched in one white-knuckled hand.

"Condemned, you mean, yellow dog of Kuur!" she hissed. "Condemned out of your own mouth, you treasonous, treacherous snake!"

Before any one of us could move or speak her hand released the blade in a blurring gesture.

The steel blade flashed across the room. But whether it struck the Mind Wizard or not, none of us could tell.

For in the same instant he vanished into thin air!

Chapter 20

Battle in the Clouds

We stared in utter amazement at the empty space which had been filled an instant before by the body of the yellow dwarf. He had flicked out of existence like an apparition, and it was a moment before any of us could grasp the fact of this miraculous disappearance. The two guards who had flanked the Kuurian shrank aside in awe and bewilderment. Even Zamara, amidst her blazing fury, was struck dumb with amazement.

Of us all, it was Ergon who first realized the truth.

"Our *minds!*" he bawled. "He's in our *minds*—get him!"

And, like a maddened tiger, the brawny, bandy-legged little colossus threw himself upon the empty air where Ang Chan had stood. There transpired an enigmatic, nightmarish battle. It was as if Ergon struggled with a tangible but unseen ghost! He seemed wrestling with the thin air itself.

Then I saw an even stranger sight—*drops of blood oozing one by one out of empty air!*

And I understood the truth behind the inexplicable phenomenon in a flash, although it took the quick wits of Ergon to realize it first. Ang Chan had not vanished—he had telepathically rendered himself· invisible. That is, using his mind-controlling powers he had made us believe he no longer stood there. And had it not been for the dagger Zamara had flung at him, which wounded him and slowed him, he would have been out the door before any of us had guessed the truth. But the blood which uncannily fell from empty air told me he was still solidly and physically there, despite my inability to see him.

Strange—strange, to see brawny Ergon bellowing lustily, struggling with empty air! But it was not empty air he was wrestling the wily and invisible Mind Wizard.

I sprang forward to lend him a hand, but the Herculean thews of the bald Perushtarian had already pinned down his invisible adversary, and even as I knelt by him, Ergon took hold of something with both strong hands and thumped it against the deck resoundingly.

And the limp form of Ang Chan melted into view again!

Panting with breath for breath, Ergon grinned up at me triumphantly.

"Mind-powers, eh?" he grunted happily. "I bethought me that if I banged the yellow man's skull against the deck a time or two, he'd lose the power to hide himself from our eyes—and there he be!"

We gathered quickly about the stunned Kuurian. His breathing was shallow and he was rapidly losing blood. Zamara's blade had caught him under the left shoulder, near his heart. His crimson gore gathered into a pool beneath him even as we watched.

"A fitting death for the treacherous dog," Zamara snarled venomously. "Let him die where he lays."

"A pity to let Ang Chan escape in death before he has answered a few questions," Darloona observed coolly. Zamara glanced at her, inquiringly. Darloona smiled.

"He could tell us much, could he not, Zamara?" she murmured. "Such as the reason why Kuur plotted to spur you to conquer the world, and what the Kuurians had hoped to gain from your victories? Or where next they planned to insinuate an agent, should they fail in their dominance of the Queen of Tharkol?"

Zamara flushed, eyes dropping. "You are right again, to my shame," she muttered. "Guards! Bind the wounds of this yellow snake and fetch the ship's doctor—"

At that instant an outcry exploded on the deck beyond our cabin and we staggered to keep our balance as the deck swung dizzily under our feet. A bugle screamed the call to quarters—the thud of running feet drummed on the deck—the snap of bowstrings twanged like plucked lutes.

"What in the name of a thousand devils is going on?" Ergon growled, scrambling to his feet. I joined him and we went out onto the deck, followed by Darloona and Zamara, leaving the Mind Wizard to the ministrations of the guards.

An amazing spectacle met our eyes!

The golden skies of Thanator were ablaze with day. Crisp clouds floated by, struck to gold by the brilliance; and there before us, sweeping grandly about as if to ram the Tharkolian airship, the mighty *Jalathadar* bore down upon us in all her grandeur. Aye, there was no mistaking her, on this occasion, for the royal colors of Shondakor fluttered from her prow and she was so near I could make out the solemn-eyed, chitinous features of Koja and the white locks of gallant Lukor in her pilothouse!

Almost in the same heartbeat of time our loyal friends recognized the crimson mane of Darloona and my own yellow locks streaming in the blaze of day and a mighty cheer went up from the decks of the *Jalathadar* at the sight of us. She trimmed her vans and came about into the wind, warriors thronged in the gunwales ready for the boarding. An instant later grappling hooks crunched into the deck rail of the *Arkonna* and the Tharkolian vessel lurched as the mass of the attacking sky ship dragged against her flight. The Tharkolian archers were already at the rail, lifting their bows, while swordsmen hacked through the grapnel lines. Another moment and battle would have been joined, there amidst the clouds.

In that desperate moment, however, Zamara revealed her true self!

"*I bid you—hold!*" she cried, her silvery voice rising like a clarion above the tumult. Springing to the rail, one hand grasping the rigging, she interposed her own body between her archers and the boarding parties. Bows were lowered as her warriors recognized their queen.

"Helmsman—strike your colors," she called and the proud ensign of Tharkol sank from view. As it fell a great shout of victory went up from the decks of the *Jalathadar* and men in the gold-and-purple livery of Royal Shondakor came swarming across the perilous lines, Koja and Lukor and young Tomar among the first of them to reach the decks of the *Arkonna.* The Tharkolians fell back to the mid-deck, yielding their arms sullenly.

And then it was that Zamara came down from the rail and strode to where we stood. Chagrin and humiliation were in her face, and tears of defeat ran down her cheeks, but her head was held proudly high and never had she looked more beautiful, or more human, than in that moment when she acknowledged her folly.

She went up to where Darloona stood and looked her straight in the face unfalteringly.

"Princess of Shondakor," she said clearly, "I have been a fool. I have made myself your enemy when I am not even worthy to be your friend. I have sinned greatly against the Crown of Shondakor without cause or reason. I yield myself into your hands. Do with me as you deem just, but spare my people who followed me into folly and madness because of loyalty and trust. I surrender myself to you, and I beg your forgiveness."

If the self-styled Empress of Callisto had never looked lovelier than in that moment of humility and surrender, never had I felt prouder of my Princess than in the moment that followed. For Darloona stepped forward and embraced Zamara and kissed her tenderly and called her friend and sister.

"Wiser heads than yours have been deluded by the cunning wiles of Kuur, my dear," she said softly. "You have the forgiveness of Shondakor for the asking, as you can have the friendship of Shondakor, if you care to ask for it."

That was a bit too much for Zamara to endure and she burst into tears. Darloona slid her arm about the slender waist of the distraught queen and led her back into the cabin so that she could compose herself in private.

And so, it seems, we had won a good friend, where we had only found an implacable enemy before.

"All's well that end's well," I said to Ergon as he came stumping up, glum-faced, to where I stood.

"If it's to be time for trite phrases, Jandar, I've one for you," he said sourly. "And that's 'dead men tell no tales.' "

"What do you mean by that?"

He cocked his head towards the cabin.

"The yellow dog of Kuur will bark no more, I fear. Zamara of Tharkol has the wrist of an assassin; I'm glad she didn't take it into her head to aim that dagger at you or me, Jandar."

And it was true. Ang Chan was dead, and with him died the untold secrets of Kuur.

"I found this under his robes, suspended about his fat neck on a thong," Ergon said glumly, handing me a small plaque of silver. I turned it over in my hand and examined it curiously. It was some sort of amulet or talisman, the gleaming metal engraved with curved and meaningless lines which trailed away at the edges of the plate. I could make nothing of it, but slipped it into my pouch to examine later at my leisure. Mayhap wise old Zastro, the sage of the Ku Thad, could spell me its meaning. There was no inscription on it that I could see.

Zamara and Darloona rejoined us a while later, and my Princess greeted Koja and Lukor and others of our friends with great happiness, introducing the Princess Zamara to them as "our ally." Zamara received their salutes in a subdued fashion but without surliness as far as I could see. I had acted more wisely than I knew, a time earlier, when at the approach of Ang Chan I had urged the wavering Empress to conceal herself behind the panel again, to listen to our conversation. It had been my hope, of course, to draw out Ang Chan in private, thinking I might get him to confirm in his own words the truth of what Darloona and I had striven to prove to Zamara. The plan, as any reader of this narrative has seen for himself, worked splendidly.

But it had been touch and go there for a few seconds! How easily all could have been lost, had Ang Chan bothered to use his telepathic powers! The most casual glance into the contents of my mind would have exposed my plan, and revealed the fact that Zamara stood concealed behind the secret panel. For some reason, thank the Lords of Gordrimator, Ang Chan had not done so . . . it may have been mere negligence, or perhaps overconfidence, or, just possibly, that my inspired burst of eloquence (if so I may term it most immodestly) had intrigued him to the neglect of caution.

But how I had sweated there for a moment or two; and how easily the roll of the dice could have gone against me. . . .

It was not a gamble I would care to risk again.

But all had worked according to my hastily contrived plan. The only drawback, of course, had been Zamara's explosion of murderous fury at discovering that the wily, smirking Kuurian had indeed tricked and deluded her cruelly, using her for his own mysterious purposes. It was a great pity she had struck down the yellow dwarf in her rage, for he could have told us much.

At any rate, having swallowed the truth in all its bitterness at last, Zamara was a changed women, and the extent of this transformation was amazing to behold. In the place of strident arrogance went soft-voiced humility. Instead of vaunting egotism she displayed quiet majesty. These new virtues, added to her undeniable vividness of character and intelligence of mind made her a stunning beauty. Darloona glowed with pride as she saw the change in Zamara reflected in the eyes of both the Tharkolian officers and the Shondakorian warriors. The poor men, being

mere men, could hardly take their eyes away from
the radiant Princess of Tharkol.

Sniveling little Glypto had maintained a rather
low profile during these swift-moving events.

Now as we stood talking on the deck, one of my
officers raised a cry, pointing below. We crowded to
the rail to see a vast procession drawn up beneath
our two ships amidst the mighty plain.

"Why, what in the world," I murmured in surprise.
"It is the caravan of Shaphur! Whatever had possessed him to follow us here . . . ?"

Looking up I caught the smiling face of Glypto.

Even as I looked an amazing change came over the
cringing little fellow.

He straightened from his habitual crouch and
stood tall, straight, and lean. The smile on his features was an honest, open grin, and not at all the
servile leer I had become accustomed to. As I
watched, speechless with surprise, he removed the
black patch, revealing an eye as bright and keen and
clear as its twin.

"Not the Lord Shaphur, I'm afraid, Prince
Jandar," he said—and the whine and whimper were
gone from his tones, leaving them firm, manly, and
deeper in timbre than before.

"Glypto?" I murmured dazedly. "Whatever do you
mean . . . ?"

"Not the merchant Shaphur, but Kaamurath,
Prince of Soraba," he said. "Whose eyes and ears in
Tharkol I have been, in all the weeks just passed
since first the Princess Zamara demanded he yield up
the sovereignty of his realm to her imperial throne!"

An expression of utter stupefaction stretched the
homely face of Ergon into a comic mask of amazement.

"I . . . you . . . w-what . . . ?" he stammered

Glypto laughed and performed a capering little
dance, sketching a parody of a bow. And for a moment the little, leering rogue we had known before
this keen-eyed, smiling stranger replaced him, stood
before us.

"Yes, friend Ergon, I fear I deceived you all! But it would have irreparably damaged my disguise had you known the whimpering little rascal you cuffed and cursed stood at the right hand of the Seraan of Soraba, and was accounted the finest swordsman in the four cities of the Perushtarian Empire," he smiled.

Ergon could only groan. It was the only time in my experience that I found him unable to think of a thing to say!

The Council of the Three Cites

The Seraan of Soraba spread huge tents amidst the grasses of the Plains of Haratha and we met in formal council within the hour.

Many minor mysteries had now been dispelled, leaving the greater mystery of Kuur unresolved.

Now I understood at last why there had been a merchant caravan on the plains where no caravan had any reason to be. The answer was that it was a military expedition, disguised as a caravan. The guards and the drivers of the wains, the outriders and the caravan beast-tenders were all seasoned and veteran Soraban warriors. And the gross merchant Shaphur was the clever and keen-witted Seraan, or Prince, of Soraba.

Alerted to danger by the insane and imperious demands of the Princess of Tharkol, Prince Kaamurath had dispatched his ablest and cleverest advisor, the master spy Glypto, to the Scarlet City. There, in the guise of a thief, Glypto had gained much intelligence regarding the imperial ambitions of Zamara. It was not, we now learned, pure chance that had led the little "thief" to our sumptuous prison-suite, but Glypto's desire to discover who we were and why we had been taken captive with such extraordinary care. Thrown in with us by the tumultuous rush of events, he had continued to play his role while observing carefully all that passed, knowing all the while that his Seraan was near, among a company of valiant warriors. And when we had fallen in with the "caravan" Glypto had been taken from us, apparently for

brutal interrogation, but actually to give his report
to his lord. The bruises he had displayed upon his
return were the result of makeup, and his whimpering terror merely the acting of a consummate artist.

For me, the most amusing of all these revelations
was the discovery that never once had Glypto actually lied to us about anything of importance!

And he actually was a *chanthan*, or mercenary adventurer, and the son and grandson of a *chanthan*
even as he had claimed at the time! It was in that capacity that he had first joined the service of the
Seraan, who rapidly promoted him to a high position because of his proven merits.

No particular friendship had ever existed between
Soraba and Shondakor; but neither had there ever
been any rancor or enmity between the two cities.
Now that it seemed we had an enemy in common, it
seemed natural to join forces against that enemy. In
this decision our newfound friend and ally, Zamara of
Tharkol, grimly vowed to do her share.

"Only by the narrowest intervention of sheer
chance were the wiles of Ang Chan of Kuur exposed
before they had caused a vast war to erupt between
the cities of Thanator," she said determinedly.

"I agree with the royal lady of Tharkol," Prince
Kaamurath said in his breathy voice. "The plots of
Kuur, which the Prince of Shondakor has just explained, imperil my realm as well as your own. Something must be done to put an end to this menace. . . ."

"Will the Seraan be willing to undertake war
against Kuur?" Darloona inquired. The fat merchant
prince puffed out his cheeks as if in indignation, then
subsided thoughtfully. For once he was not gobbling
sweetmeats and gulping wine: hard, practical, and
serious was this Perushtarian monarch, surprisingly
different from his brother rulers.

As if he, too, possessed the power to read minds,
and had somehow sensed the tenor of my thoughts,
he spoke out in thoughtful, measured tones.

"We of Perushtar, I know, are often thought un-
warlike, more concerned with our purses than with

honor," he said. "In some measure there is truth in this, but not entirely. There comes a time when only war will serve the needs of the realm; men must be willing to fight against aggression, if there is to be peace. And trade and commerce flourish best when peace exists between kingdoms. Thus, upon my accession, I assembled and trained a host of warriors, which is something no Seraan of Perushtar has done before my reign."

This was quite true, of course. Previously, the Princes of Perushtar had purchased the service of that host of mercenary warriors, the Black Legion, to fight their battles for them. But since the Ku Thad succeeded in breaking the Legion, the custom fell into disuse, there being no longer any Black Legion to hire. And in another way Kaamurath of Soraba differed from his fellow princes; generally the Seraans of Perushtar are powerless puppets, and the reins of power are firmly grasped by the wealthy merchant clans who dominate the oligarchic state. But Kaamurath had somehow won the support of the great merchant princes, using a coalition of their strength as the base of his power. He was a rare individual in the Perushtarian Empire, and a valuable ally to have with us in any war against Kuur.

"Shondakor agrees," Darloona said in return, "but will Soraba fight with us, or merely stand by while Tharkol and Shondakor carry the battle alone?"

Prince Kaamurath gave her a long, level look, and then smiled grimly. "Princess, we will stand with you in this endeavor. For no man can say where next the Mind Wizards will seek to spin their plots—mayhap in mine own realm! For that very good and very practical reason, Soraba suggests we take the initiative and carry the war into Kuur itself."

"But who knows where the kingdom of the Mind Wizards is?" asked Zamara.

"The information I had from the lips of Ool the Uncanny," I said, "was that the kingdom of the Mind Wizards is concealed somewhere on the other side of this planet. It is common knowledge that those lands are uncharted and unexplored, doubtless for the simple reason that no travelers have ever been permitted to return from those lands. Thus we may expect to find the Mind Wizards maintain some manner of surveillance over the roads that lead unto their hidden and secret realm."

"The skies of Thanator are a road no warrior can guard," Zamara said. "I will place my ships, the *Arkonna* and the *Conqueress,* under your command, Prince Jandar, if you will. And I will fill those ships with the noblest and most skilled and valiant fighting-men of Tharkol!"

"To which we will add our vessels, the *Xaxar* and the *Jalathadar,*" Darloona added, "which will be manned by the finest warriors of Shondakor. Our combined fleets will comprise the mightiest war fleet upon the planet. Kuur shall reel and crumble beneath our combined assault!"

"And, for my part, I will drain the coffers of Soraba," said Kaamurath, "to outfit the four galleons of the skies with the finest weapons that may be purchased. Food and drink and supplies of every kind will Soraba give to this expedition, and our most knowledgeable explorers and navigators, map makers and geographers, will be at your command."

And so it was decided, and swiftly. Never again would we let the cunning yellow men of mysterious Kuur gain the upper hand.

From this moment, although they knew it not, we were at war against them.

For our real enemies had never been ourselves. Tharkol was no enemy to Soraba, nor to Shondakor.

Our secret and hidden enemies all the time had been the Mind Wizards of Callisto!

And now, at last, the veils were stripped away from our eyes, and we saw things clearly. And as I sat there in the tent amidst the Plains of Haratha, I vowed within my heart that never should I rest until this last and greatest threat to the peace of the Jungle Moon should be crushed in blood and flame.

I would lead the greatest expedition ever launched across the borders of the known surface of Thanator into an unknown and mysterious world. And there, in secret and shadowy Kuur, I would cross swords at last with my deadliest adversaries—the dreadful and sinister Mind Wizards of Callisto!

And in the battle I would either emerge the victor or go down to a miserable death.

The Beasts of Thanator

At this point in the publication of several volumes of the journals of Jonathan Andrew Dark, quite a considerable amount of random information has been given us concerning the strange and unusual beasts, reptiles, and monsters which roam the surface of remote and mysterious Callisto, fly in her weird golden skies, or swim in her landlocked seas.

While editing Captain Dark's manuscripts for publication in this series I have been gathering notes on the many peculiar and remarkable lifeforms he has thus far encountered during his adventures on this distant and unknown planet. These notes I offer to you here, by way of attempting to systematize the data a study of his journals reveals.

Lin Carter

THE GLOSSARY

ARGANG

A shellfish found in the waters of the Corund Laj from whose "marrow" a delicious paste is made. A gourmet delicacy prized particularly by the Perushtarians; Jandar compares its flavor to that of caviar. *Note:* Since marrow is a substance found in bones, and since shellfish like clams and oysters have no skeletons, I frankly don't understand what he means by saying the delicacy is prepared from the "marrow" of these crustaceans. The word "marrow" may perhaps be an error in translation.

BORATH

A kind of tree common to the jungles of Thanator. Jandar describes it as having "gnarled and twisted" branches, knotted into fantastic shapes, and "unlike any terrene trees" familiar to him. The wood of the *borath* is jet black, its foliage crimson. The fact that the leaves of the *borath* are crimson must mean there is no chlorophyll in them, which makes it difficult to understand how such plants could thrive; Jandar, however, tells us in several places that the leaves and grasses of Callisto are uniformly crimson. Since Callisto receives little or no sunlight, due to its extreme distance from the sun, the Callistan vegetation must employ some unique method of producing carbohydrates other than photosynthesis.

DELTAGAR

A terrible predator of the Thanatorian jungles which Jandar describes as a "super-tiger" with scarlet fur and a lashing whiplike tail edged with sharp serrations. Its brow is armed with two curling horns and its jaws contain great canine fangs like that of the extinct saber-toothed tiger.

FOMAK

Venomous cave-spiders found on the far side of Callisto, and perhaps unique to that hemisphere. Here we anticipate the fifth volume of these journals, *Mind Wizards of Callisto*, still in preparation.

GHASTOZAR

A dreaded flying reptile of enormous size, rapacious hunger, difficult to slay, and large enough to be ridden by men. Jandar compares the batwinged sky dragon of Callisto to the prehistoric pterodactyl.

GLYMPH

A heavy, lumbering, oxlike beast of burden employed by the Callistans as a draft animal. Jandar describes it as resembling a rhinoceros or a kind of dinosaur called the triceratops, which had a capacious bony shield protecting its neck and numerous horns. Its hide is slate gray, turning to a yellowish hue at throat and belly; Jandar adds that nature, for some inscrutable reason of her own "has seen fit to ornament the imposing creatures with tiger-stripes of an amazing shade of crimson." This may be a form of protective coloration, designed to help conceal the *glymph* from its enemies in the Thanatorian jungles, for, as we have seen in the entry under BORATH, the Callistan jungle foliage is also crimson. (This is only a guess on my part, since Jandar does not indicate the jungle country as the natural habitat of the *glymph*.)

HARTHAK

Immense, man-eating giant clams found along the coasts of the Corund Laj. Divers of the Perushtarian cities would seem to hunt these monster clams for the gigantic pearls sometimes found within them, from a remark quoted in the present volume.

HOREB

Jandar describes this beast as a repulsive scavenger of loathsome eating habits. I suppose the *horeb* to be a large rodent; at any rate the author of these journals tells us the word is employed by the Thanatorians as an insulting or derogatory word, as we use the word *rat*.

JARUKA

Another kind of tree found commonly in the jungle country; like the *borath* it has crimson foliage, trunk, and branches and roots of fantastically gnarled and knotted black wood. Jandar does not specify any particular difference between the two trees, except to remark in at least one place that, of the two, the *borath* is the taller.

JINKO

The amazing "walking trees" of Callisto: a unique and very peculiar perambulating bush which sometimes attains the size of a small tree, and which progresses from place to place across the Haratha Plains and in the desert country seeking water. Sensing itself near to a subterranean source of water, the *jinko* pauses at the site, inserts its roots into the ground and, as it were, takes aboard a supply of drinkables, which it stores in hollow bladder-like leaves. The *jinko* seems to possess some rudimentary degree of intelligence and possesses as well the wit to flee from beasts and men of the Plains, which hunt it for its unique and valuable water-storing properties, as a sort of ambulating oasis. A friend of mine, an experienced naturalist, assures me no earthly form of plant life possesses anything like the abilities of the fantastic *jinko*.

LAJAZELL

A small winged reptile which is commonly found along the shores of the two inland seas of Callisto. The prefix *laja* ("sea") serves to differentiate the creature from its desert-dwelling cousin. See ZELL.

OTHODE

A large, heavily built wild animal of the jungle country with a supple, leathery hide of a remarkable purple hue, a waddling, six-legged stride, and an ugly, neckless head with goggling eyes and a wide, froglike mouth armed with blunt and powerful tusks. Here again I anticipate the publication of *Mind Wizards of Callisto*; for in that volume of these journals, the *othode* is described as being about the size and weight of a bull mastiff, and no less ferocious. The brutes are highly intelligent, however, and are sometimes domesticated for hunting or guarding purposes, if seldom as house pets. Jandar describes them as remarkably doglike in their faithfulness, loyalty, and capacity for affection and love.

SORAD

A very rare species of tree seldom found on Callisto, and held in a kind of superstitious veneration due to this rarity by certain of the less civilized nations of Callisto, such as the Yathoon barbarians. Its uniqueness lies in its coloration, for it reverses the usual red foliage and black wood of the more common *borath* and *jaruka* trees, having red wood and black leaves.

THAPTOR

The marvelous gryphons or "bird-horses" of Callisto, a wingless but befeathered four-legged creature used by the Thanatorians as a riding steed. They have a rufflike mane of stiff bristling feathers, clawed feet armed with roosterlike spurs, and sharp yellow beaks like parrots. Domesticated with great difficulty, the *thaptors* are unruly and vicious. They also seem to be the only avian species found on the entire planet, the winged lifeforms being reptilian, so far as these journals inform us.

VANTH

A beast of the Great Plains which rather closely resembles in size and in its crest of antlers the earthly elk or stag. Instead of fur, the *vanth* is covered with a slick, supple hide like that of a seal or dolphin. The quadrupeds are greatly prized for their meat.

VASTODON

The mighty "elephant-boar" of the Grand Kumala jungles, which resembles a miniature pachyderm with its thick, columnar legs ending in flat pads, barrel-shaped body and gray, leathery hide. The proboscis is covered with coarse bristles and has some resemblance to a pig's snout, but attains the length of three feet or so, which enhances its elephantine appearance. Hunted by the Yathoon for its meat, the *vastodon* is a vicious fighter.

XANGA

A peculiar, quasi-intelligent kind of insect domesticated by the Yathoon arthropods. About the size of a small dog, these androgynous creatures possess bee-like stingers charged with a peculiar paralysis-inducing venom.

XLMCHAK

Repulsive, enormous spiders which haunt certain portions of the Grand Kumala and from whose immense webs a tough, elastic substance like silk, but stronger than nylon, is prepared.

YATHRIB

The terrific "dragon-cat" of the jungle country, feared as one of the most dangerous predators of Callisto. Jandar describes the *yathrib* as an unlikely cross between a gigantic tiger and a dragonlike reptile, its sinuous catlike body and gliding, steely thews sheathed in glittering emerald scales which pale to tawny yellow at the belly plates. Its feet are armed

with terrible, razor-sharp bird claws capable of
disemboweling a full-grown *deltagar* in a single
stroke, and its backbone is protected by a jagged
row of horny plates which extend the length of its
body to the barbed tip of its snaky tail. Because it is
indestructible due to its double brain, the Yathoon
use a deadly nerve poison against it, dipping their ar-
rowheads and the blades of their spears in a distilla-
tion of spider venom.

ZELL

Small winged reptiles found in the desert country, a
species similar to the *lajazell* of the shores of the
Corund Laj. Generally regarded as harmless—much as
we, for instance, regard seagulls—they hunt in enormous flocks and can strip a human being to the naked
bones in a few seconds. In *Mind Wizards of Callisto,* Jandar describes them as a sort of Jekyll-and-
Hyde creature, "half seagull, half bat-winged pira-
nha."

ZULTH

A repulsive, garbage-eating scavenger not unlike the
horeb, but a small reptile rather than a rodent.

These twenty-one species of Callistan animal or reptile or plant life are all Jandar refers to by name in
those five volumes of his journals we have yet received.

He does, however, make certain other references
at various places in the books on which he does not
expand. There is, for example, a kind of beast which
was formerly used against men in the gladiatorial are-
na of Zanadar, to which he alludes in the first volume
of these memoirs, *Jandar of Callisto.* The entry to
which I refer may be found on page 171 of that
book: "They were a collection of oddly shaped crea- ·
tures—scaled reptilian predators with long snakelike
necks, who bounded about on huge hind legs in fantastic leaps like midget tyrannosaurs crossed in some
unlikely mating with giant kangaroos." This would
seem to be the only mention of these particular
beasts anywhere in the five volumes of these memoirs

I have yet seen; I cannot list them alphabetically in the Glossary, as he nowhere refers to them by name, but I include their description here for the sake of completeness.

In much the same way, the present volume, *Red Empress of Callisto*, makes a passing reference to "the great dragon-fish of the Corund Laj." That's all Jandar has to say about the creature, and he nowhere to my knowledge gives it any name.

These notes, then, comprise the sum total of our present knowledge of the several and peculiar lifeforms indigenous to Callisto, moon of Jupiter.

—Lin Carter

www.ingramcontent.com/pod-product-compliance
Lightning Source LLC
Chambersburg PA
CBHW032009240626
47153CB00003B/1187